Near Miss

THE GALLOPING DETECTIVE
BOOK SIX

Near Miss

CLAIRE BIRCH

A YEARLING BOOK

Published by
Dell Publishing
a division of
Bantam Doubleday Dell Publishing Group, Inc.
666 Fifth Avenue
New York, New York 10103

The trademark Yearling® is registered in the U.S. Patent and Trademark Office.

The trademark Dell® is registered in the U.S. Patent and Trademark Office.

ISBN: 0-440-40557-2

RL: 4.9
Ages 9–13

Printed in the United States of America

January 1992

10 9 8 7 6 5 4 3 2

OPM

To Helen-Ann and Alex,
the best of neighbors and friends

Chapter One

"Look, Allison, he just stands there!" Lucy pointed to a sea gull at the end of the ferry slip. The gray, weatherbeaten pilings creaked and groaned as the small ferry moved the girls away from shore, but the bird only turned his head.

"He's looking us over," Allison said, smoothing her long hair.

Lucy waved. "Good-bye, bird." She rested her suitcase against her feet and scanned the bay between Greenpoint and Shelby Island. "That gull's the *only* thing in the harbor that isn't moving." To the right a large powerboat left a foaming white trail. Nearby a flock of sailboats bobbed up and down on a sequence of waves.

Allison threw back her shoulders. "Smell the sea," she ordered.

Lucy filled her lungs with the salt air and squinted at the island about a quarter of a mile away. Several rambling houses were almost completely hidden by large trees along the shoreline. Her breath escaped in a sigh.

"It's fantastic here, Allison. But I can't get it through my head that it's *me* standing on this ferry. I really expected to be back in Connecticut for July."

"Well, you'll be there a month later and in the meantime you'll have fun. Shelby Island may be a dot on the map, but it's a great place and the Mosedales are a blast."

"It's the riding I'm thinking of, and you know it. If I don't move ahead this summer, I might as well give up on the Maclay." As Lucy looked off to the right, where the open water stretched on and on, the National Horse Show seemed very far away. But to ride in the Maclay Finals at the National had been her ambition since the age of ten. Now that she was sixteen, she'd be eligible for only two more years.

"I thought the Mosedales said you could show one of their horses while you're here."

"They did. But I don't know what the horse will be like or how much free time I'll have to train. Besides, I miss Mr. Kendrick, and after a winter away from Up and Down Farm, I counted on riding with him again."

Allison tossed her head. "It will do you good to be on your own. Mr. Kendrick's like some kind of a guru—"

"That's ridiculous. He's just a great trainer who's been a big influence in my life."

Allison stared at the shore. "Okay, put it your way. But there's more to summer than riding. I could teach you to sail."

Lucy lifted her damp brown hair off her neck. She took off her sunglasses and wiped the perspiration from around her eyes. In its true colors, the island seemed to glow.

Allison pointed to a large white house in the distance. "That's the yacht club. Most Shelby Island kids learn to sail there, but my dad taught me. He's the best."

"How long have you been coming out here?"

"Forever. We've had the house since before I was born. My father and Austin Mosedale were at college together and Dad used to visit in the summer. When they grew up, Dad and another college friend—Arthur Haddem—bought houses of their own."

"I'm glad to be staying with you tonight," Lucy said. "I can see your parents and catch up with myself before I meet the Mosedales." She turned to Allison. "Please don't misunderstand. I'm really excited about this job, and I'm lucky you told me about it."

"I hope you'll still say that after mucking out six stalls every day."

"What do I care? I'll be in charge of a whole barn by myself—well, almost." Lucy smiled. "I realize Mr. Mosedale's sister has the final say about the horses. Have you seen the kids ride?"

"No, but the older ones, Kit and Glenn junior, have been out here three summers, so they're probably pretty good."

"And James? The little boy I'm supposed to fix up?"

"I don't know much about him. He came for the first time last July when I was away." She scanned the road behind the ferry house in the distance. "I don't see the Cherokee, but my mother always makes it down the hill before we get there."

Lucy looked over the rail and watched the ferry carve a ridge into the water. It was funny the way things worked out. Last summer, when she'd found out about her parents breaking up, she'd been sure she'd never live through it. And moving to New York with her mother last fall had been the worst of all. But Allison had turned up in her new school and you couldn't want a better friend. Then she'd worried about not being able to ride at a good-enough stable, but in the spring she'd commuted to Oak Ridge in Westchester. What's more, she'd met Ken there—the brother of her favorite riding pupil.

Lucy glanced at her watch. A real improvement! She hadn't thought of Ken for at least three hours.

The ferry thumped into its berth and the roar of car motors started behind them. Allison nudged Lucy's arm. "Let's go. Passengers get off first."

Lucy picked up her suitcase as the ferryman unhooked a large white chain. Near the ferry house Allison's mother waved from her car.

I feel miles away from everywhere, Lucy thought as she stepped ashore. But an island had always seemed a mysterious and romantic place, one that held secrets apart from the rest of the world. Would Shelby Island be anything like that?

● ● ●

"I understand that your mother's in Italy," Mrs. Barker said as Lucy and Allison sat in matching wicker chairs on the Barkers' screen porch. The evening light was a gentle pink and the water of the bay had lost its glitter.

"Yes, *City and Country* needed a writer at the last minute for an article on European music festivals. We had to postpone moving back to Connecticut, but it was too good an assignment to turn down."

"And your father's a TV producer, isn't he?"

"Yes. He's making thirteen new episodes of *Malibu* in California."

Allison said, "That's the show Lucy worked on during spring vacation. You remember, when she was doing the stunt riding."

Mr. Barker swung through the door from the living room. "Hello, ladies." He was a tall man with powerful shoulders and blue eyes as bright as neon. "Welcome aboard, Lucy. We haven't seen you since the end of school."

"Hi, Mr. Barker. It's good to be here. I hope I'll get a chance to visit while I'm working."

"You will, I'm sure. You'll do fine over there. The Mosedale clan's not a bad lot." He winked at Allison. "You might even strike it rich!"

"Come on, Dad. Lucy's not going to fall for that old story."

Lucy sat forward in her chair. "Tell me! What story?"

Allison shrugged. "Austin's father bought their house in the 1930s. They used to call it the 'Treasure House' because of Judge Trabert, the former owner. He was a big shot during Prohibition days and in the end the mob got rid of him."

"All that happened here—on this quiet little island?"

Mr. Barker held up a hand. "Go back some, Allison. Shelby Island was a perfect spot for rum runners from 1920 to 1933—the years when alcohol was illegal in the United States. Here it sat, sheltered between the two fingers of Long Island. The big ships from Cuba could anchor out there beyond the three-mile limit, nice and legal. Then their speedboats raced the booze past the

Coast Guard to our Shelby Island coves. Judge Trabert collected the liquor so it could be moved into the speak-easies in New York. He pulled some kind of a fast one and ended up in a coffin."

"Where does 'treasure' come into it?" Lucy asked.

"When the judge died they found stacks of money stashed all over the house. Either he didn't trust banks or he was planning to leave the country in a hurry. People like to think there's still more cash in the house some-where."

"I know you love to solve mysteries, but no one's found any since," Allison said. "Don't get your hopes up."

Lucy grinned. "I'll settle for the money I'm earning. It's much more than I expected."

"That's because they were lucky to get someone on such short notice." Mrs. Barker smiled at Lucy. "Some-one with riding and teaching experience too. Most peo-ple have made their summer plans by the end of June."

"Why did the Mosedales wait so long?" Lucy asked.

"It was only last week that they found out James would be here again—and without his mother. He's only eight—"

"The caretaker was fired too," Allison interrupted. "They need someone to help Susannah Mosedale at the stable."

"Is the whole family there at once? It seems like a lot of people for Mr. Mosedale to have around for the sum-mer."

Mr. Barker laughed. "Austin hasn't any choice. The Old Bull Moose—Austin's father, Archer Mosedale—left the place to his five children. They all have equal rights, although Austin manages the family business. He runs the house, too, from what I understand."

"Five owners?" Lucy counted on her fingers. "I know about Mr. Mosedale and his sister, Susannah, but who are the other three?"

"There's Dr. Mosedale, the father of Kit and Glenn junior," Allison said, "and there's Katherine, James's mother."

"That's only *four*," Lucy said.

"Oh, I didn't tell you about Brett."

"Brett?"

"He's the oldest cousin—"

"How old?"

"Twenty-four . . . and bad news. He—"

"That kid's embarrassed Austin all over the island," Mr. Barker cut in. "He collects speeding tickets on land and on sea. He's been banned at the country club for getting into fights. Brett's one nasty boy when he drinks."

"Come on, Dad. He's not all bad," Allison said quickly. "Anyway, Lucy, Brett's parents died in a plane crash when he was three and he inherited their share. You'll see him racing around in one gorgeous car or another. He's spoiled rotten."

"How will I ever keep all these characters straight?" Lucy said, forcing a laugh.

Mrs. Barker was looking at her closely. "Lucy's had enough of the Mosedales for now," she said. "Let's talk about something else."

"Not yet, Mom. Look who's coming."

A girl and a boy, about ten and twelve, were walking

toward the porch. "Hello, Mrs. Barker," they chorused. "We came over to meet Lucy."

"Well, here she is," Allison said.

The girl approached Lucy formally and put out a hand. "I'm Katherine Talbot Mosedale and I love horses the way you do." She was an appealing girl with eyes the color of a caramel candied apple. Her short hair, which matched her eyes exactly, was pulled to one side in a green barrette.

"She's called Kit. I'm Glenn. Glenn junior," the tall boy said. His hair and eyes were just like his sister's.

Lucy felt suddenly buoyant. These looked like two nice kids. It should be fun to teach them riding. Even keeping an eye on them would probably be easy.

"When are you coming to our house?" Kit asked.

"In the morning."

"What time? Seven o'clock?"

Lucy smiled. "More like eight or nine."

"Ralph, the caretaker, is gone," Glenn said. "If you got there early, you could help with the stable."

What did that mean? Were they just eager to have her join them or was Glenn giving her orders?

"I'll drive Lucy over around nine," Allison said firmly.

Kit looked at her feet. "Don't you want to see Susannah's horse, Golden Toy?"

"And Radar? He's beautiful!"

"Of course I do. But Allison and I are good friends and we haven't had a real chance to talk since school ended last month. I'll be over at nine o'clock on the dot and you'll show me all the horses first thing."

Mrs. Barker motioned toward a wicker table. "Would

you like some peanuts? Or some cheese and crackers? By the way, where's James?"

"You mean 'Bean'? He's home labeling bugs," Glenn said. "He catches them off the kitchen screen door at night. Are you going to teach him to ride, Lucy?"

"That's part of my agreement with your uncle. I'm planning on it."

Glenn joined Kit at the cheese board. "Good luck," he said. "Last summer Bean didn't get on a horse once."

• • •

Lucy pulled a nightgown out of her suitcase, along with the print cosmetic case her mother had given her. From the bedroom window the scattered lights across the harbor looked like tiny nailheads hammered into the darkness. Somewhere the water from that bay out there would reach the open sea and somewhere at the end of it all was Ken. Why did his mother have to live in England? And why did he have to visit her each summer?

"Hey, dreamy eyes, have you heard from Ken yet?" Allison said.

"Are you reading my mind?"

Allison sat down on the edge of her bed in an oversized night shift. "If Ken Peister were my boyfriend, I'd think about him all the time."

Lucy studied Allison as she leaned back on the bed. Other people just moved around, but Allison arranged herself in positions, like a model, and looked sensational in anything she wore.

"I haven't had a letter yet," Lucy said, "but Ken's only been gone one week, one day, and—eight hours.

I've been meaning to ask you, how often does mail get delivered to this island?"

"Every morning. You drive to the post office for it."

"Allison," Lucy wailed. "You know I can't drive. Mom was going to teach me when we moved back to Connecticut. Can I bike to the post office?"

"Sure, if your legs hold up. But people are always going back and forth to the village."

As Allison went into the bathroom, Lucy reached for the green notebook in which she'd started a summer journal. On the first page she'd drawn a freehand calendar to keep track of the days until Ken came home. She crossed off the day's date and wondered what time it was in London. Was Ken thinking about her too? It was hard to believe she'd only met him a few months ago. So much had happened. Ken's father was a famous violinist and when his priceless Stradivarius violin disappeared, she'd been able to solve the mystery. She'd heard a recording by Mr. Peister on the radio the other day but it had been hard to listen; the music reminded her that Ken was so far away.

Suddenly Lucy felt terribly alone. What was she doing on Shelby Island? But there was no way she could have turned down this job at the Mosedales'. She couldn't stay by herself while her mother was away. And she felt uncomfortable about going to her father. She liked his girlfriend, Lynne, but Lucy couldn't stop hoping that her parents would get together again. Then, too, she'd make money at the Mosedales that she needed for horse shows, in August. Her parents stretched hard to pay all the expenses for her riding, even though she worked off some lessons by teaching beginners.

Lucy closed her journal with the first page still blank. Had she been too confident in accepting this job? She'd disappoint the Barkers as well as the Mosedales if it didn't work out. She'd never taken care of kids all day before. And winning over a reluctant eight-year-old was different from teaching kids who couldn't wait to ride. Six horses were a cinch if they all stayed healthy, but there were no guarantees. Only one thing was really clear: She might not have time to work on her *own* riding. That sixth blue ribbon Over Fences that she needed, the one that would finally make her an Open Rider working toward the Maclay, could easily get lost in the shuffle.

Allison came back into the room. "Don't worry about your mail tomorrow. I'll be sure to pick up whatever's there."

"No one will ever have a better friend than *you*, Allison—even if you did hold out on me about Brett!"

Lucy stretched out on her bed and caught the smell of seaweed in the air. It had been silly to feel alone with Allison on the island. As for the rest of her worries, she'd learned a lot about the unexpected this year in New York, and it hadn't all been bad. She'd just take the month on Shelby Island a day at a time and see what surprises turned up.

Chapter Two

Lucy and Allison drove along the causeway that connected the main part of Shelby Island to a smaller bit of land called Stag's Head. There were strips of pebbled beach on both sides of the tarred road and a steep hill ahead.

"Stag's Head has always been my favorite part of Shelby," Allison said. "There are big old houses like the Mosedales' all along the water and yet the center is still mostly all woods." She pointed up ahead. "Look, a welcoming committee."

Three small figures stood like statues at the top of the hill until Allison yelled, "Hi, kids." She stopped the car beside them and all three rushed to Lucy's window.

"Hi, you guys," Lucy said. Her eyes glanced off Kit and Glenn junior to a skinny blond boy beside them.

"I'm Bean," the boy said, looking into Lucy's face with huge gray eyes.

"I'm glad to meet you, Bean."

The boy looked down at the road and wound one skinny leg around the other.

"We're ready to ride, see?" Kit pointed to the leather paddock boots below her blue jeans. Glenn, too, wore low boots, but Bean was in sneakers.

"Hop in," Allison ordered. The kids were already scrambling into the backseat.

"That's Stag's Head Inn," Kit volunteered as they turned right.

"Our place starts after the inn," Glenn said, "and goes way down on both sides. Too bad Willy's not out to welcome you, but there's no one to clean up after him since Ralph's gone."

"Willy?"

"He's a Shetland pony that belongs to Brett," Bean said solemnly. "He looks like chocolate. Did you ever read *Willy Wonka and the Chocolate Factory*?"

Lucy turned to Allison. "Am I getting mixed up? I thought Brett was the twenty-four-year-old who's . . ." She swallowed "bad news" just in time.

Kit suppressed a giggle. "Aunt Susannah bought Willy when Brett was a little kid."

"Lucy, what horse are *you* going to ride?" Bean asked.

"Your uncle said Radar."

Had she imagined the quick look between Kit and Glenn? The kids fell silent.

"We'd like to show you the stables," Kit said finally, "but Aunt Susannah's waiting down by the house. Can you see her?"

Lucy followed Kit's eyes to a tall figure standing at the head of the driveway near a circle of shrubs. Behind her was a sprawling house of brown weathered shingles. What was it going to be like to live in a house that big?

Allison pulled up in front of a four car garage. The car had barely stopped when Bean ran off toward Susannah shouting, "She's here!"

"Don't mind him," Glenn said. "He's still a baby." He reached for Lucy's suitcase. "Hey, I should be carrying that."

Kit walked beside Lucy. "Bean *is* a baby about horses. But not about everything. He swims better than all of us. I guess you *could* say his head's in the clouds a lot of the time. That's what Uncle Austin keeps saying."

Across the driveway the tall woman advanced toward them with a powerful stride. She was big boned, with a broad jaw and a large, straight nose, but her face was somehow handsome and, like Bean's, a setting for large gray eyes.

"Good morning, Allison."

"Good morning, Susannah. Well, here she is! Lucy Hill, special delivery."

Kit looked up at Lucy. "Your eyes are positively green!"

"Kit Mosedale, we don't make personal remarks," Susannah said. She studied Lucy in silence, and Lucy thought she'd prefer Kit's spontaneous remarks any day.

"I'm glad you've come," Susannah said finally. "Let's show Lucy the house and grounds. Then we'll go to the stables."

Allison said with a wry smile, "Since you're satisfied, Susannah, I'll take off."

Lucy reached out to stop her, then dropped her hand quickly. "When will I see you?"

"Don't worry. I'll check in." Allison waved and walked to her car.

"Come!" Susannah said. "Leave the suitcase on the steps for now and we'll show Lucy the grounds." She led the way around one end of the house. "This is the bedroom wing. My room is upstairs next to Mr. and Mrs. Mosedale. Your room, Lucy, is on the ground floor next to Kit and the two boys."

Where did Brett live, then? Maybe there was an apartment over the garage.

"Will I meet Mr. Mosedale today?" Lucy asked, suppressing her real question.

"Austin's in Delaware with his wife, Jane." Susannah paused. "Why don't you use our first names, Lucy? I think that will be best. In any case, Jane will be away for some time because her mother broke her hip. Austin should be back tomorrow."

When they reached the back of the house, Lucy caught her breath. Tiger lilies blazed a line of fire behind the stone wall that separated the lawn from the beach. Across the large sheltered harbor a single house and dock was the only break in a line of tall trees.

"You're looking at Sailors Harbor," Susannah announced.

Kit pointed. "That's Haddem's house on the edge of the nature preserve. He comes over here a lot."

The third college friend, Lucy thought, remembering what Allison had said on the ferry—Allison's father, Haddem, and Austin Mosedale.

As they trooped toward the Mosedales' dock, Lucy spotted a fiberglass rowboat pulled up on the beach.

"Do you row?" she asked the cousins.

"Not in that boat," Bean said. "No one touches that boat but Uncle Austin." There was an edge to his voice.

At the end of the dock a shingled boathouse matched the house. A large motorboat with a flying bridge was tied up nearby. Lucy squinted against the sunlight to read the name on its stern. "The *Gismo*?"

"It's something to do with the business our great-grandfather started . . . and how it got real big. . . ."

"Glenn's right," Susannah said. "Grandpa made Mosedale Products a solid business, but Austin turned it into Mosedale Industries, a major corporation. One important reason was a little piece of metal that goes into almost every safety brake made. Austin always called that little device 'the gismo.'"

"My uncle's nuts about his boat and he really likes to fish," Glenn said. "You can come with us sometime."

"Terrific."

Lucy turned back toward the enormous house. The bedrooms were balanced by a wing at the opposite end where some kind of construction was going on. Along the center of the house a long screened porch opened onto a stone patio. A flagpole nearby reminded Lucy of summer camp.

"We're extending the dining room and the wine cellar," Susannah said at Lucy's shoulder. "That explains the bricks and tarpaulins over there."

Glenn said brusquely, "No one's working again this morning." Lucy tried not to smile. Was she hearing an echo of Uncle Austin?

"Amos must have gone off to some other job, but he'll be back," Susannah said. "He's been the only contractor on the island for years and everyone needs him. Well, now, I think we should let Lucy unpack, don't you?

Come and get me when you're ready to go up to the barn."

Finally alone in her room, Lucy looked around eagerly. She should be comfortable enough here, even though the furniture was the simplest maple and the walls a dreary knotty pine. Luckily, an upholstered chair and a flowered bedspread with matching curtains added some color.

"Are you almost ready?" Kit called from behind the door.

"Not yet, Kit, in about ten minutes."

Lucy put her clothes away quickly. She stacked her tapes next to her tape deck on the bureau, lined up her veterinary and Pony Club manuals on the table along with the books she'd brought along to read. At first she left her green journal on the table, too, but on second thought put it in a drawer. She just didn't feel at home enough yet to leave it out in the open.

"Lucy?" This time Glenn was at the door. "Are you ready? We can't find Bean. I'll bet he was afraid you'd make him ride."

"Hold on a minute," she said, stepping into her breeches. She pulled on her old black boots, grabbed her hard hat, and opened the door.

"We've looked all the places Bean usually hides, but he's picked a new one this time."

Kit had come into the hallway. "He's not in the boathouse cupboard. Hey, Glenn, Brett left his outboard motor on the dock again. Uncle Austin's going to have fits."

Lucy stopped to think. Where would she hide around here?

"Come on, kids. I've an idea." She led the way to the wine cellar. The dark tarpaulin, stretched over the new bricks, made a low, tentlike shape close to the ground.

"Bean, I know you're under there," Lucy announced. "Come on out. We're all waiting for you."

There wasn't the tiniest ripple under the tarp. Had she been wrong?

"Bean, I promise you. I won't make you ride today, but we can't go up to the stable without you."

"Yeah, Bean," Glenn said.

A small lump distorted the smooth rubber surface. It traveled toward the edge and turned into a small head with big ears. Bean crawled into the open and stood in front of Lucy. At the sight of his cousins his grin disappeared. One hand went into his shirt pocket, then quickly moved up to his ear.

"Let's go," Lucy said, and led the way to the front of the house.

Susannah stood at the steps, elegant in pale gray Kentucky breeches and a matching shirt. "In all the excitement about Lucy, do you know what we forgot?"

"The sailing placement tests," Glenn said. "I didn't forget."

Kit snapped, "Because you'd rather sail than ride."

"You're due there at twelve o'clock," Susannah said, "so if you want to ride even half an hour, you'll have to hurry." As they started up the driveway, she added sharply, "Where are your boots, Bean?"

"Miss Mosedale—" Lucy broke in.

"Susannah!"

"Susannah, could I please talk to you about Bean's

lessons before he has to ride? I know we'll be going over the stable routine and maybe then—"

Susannah silenced Lucy with her critical stare. After several moments she said, "All right. But I warn you, Lucy, Austin's mind is made up about getting Bean on a horse."

"I understand," Lucy answered slowly.

What kind of a man was Austin Mosedale, anyway? What difference did it make if Bean *never* got on a horse? Why was this so important?

Bean stayed close to Lucy while Susannah strode ahead with Glenn and Kit. He took a funny little skip every so often to help keep up.

"Look!" Bean said. "They put fences around the baby trees so the deer won't eat the bark."

"Deer walk around here just like that?"

"A lot of times. Once I got close enough to touch one. A doe all by herself. She stood real still while I tiptoed up very quietly, but then Ralph started his Jeep."

So! Bean wasn't afraid of *all* animals.

"I'd love to see a deer on the lawn here," Lucy said, "especially with a fawn."

"I'll keep watching for you." He ran ahead to his cousins. "We've got to look out for some deer for Lucy. Be sure to tell her if you see any." Then he stood still until she caught up.

"Bean, which horse do you like best?" Lucy asked.

"Jonah, I guess. He looks like brown leather that's been rubbed a lot."

"Have you ridden Jonah?"

"I don't ride horses."

They crossed the tar road and walked through the

woods a short way to a clearing. The small green-and-white stable, surrounded by a circular paddock, looked more like a perfect toy model than a barn in use every day. The six horses grazing nearby looked well cared for. Lucy recognized Jonah from Bean's description, and, of course, the pony, Willy Wonka. But which was Radar? And where was the three-gaited saddle horse? Susannah had said that she never rode hunters.

Kit led the way past a riding ring to an enclosed field of grass on the other side of the barn. "That's 'Susannah's Golden Toy,'" she said. A light chestnut trotted by, head arched, tail and mane flying. "Isn't he the most spectacular horse you've ever seen?"

"Remember, we have to hurry," Susannah said. "Catch your horses, clean them up, and get into the ring. I'll be right back." She walked off calling to Toy.

"It's hard to believe all this is hidden away back here," Lucy said.

"Isn't it great! We've even got trails winding through the woods. Aunt Susannah had it all built. She says she believes in spending her money, not hoarding it like some people."

Kit and Glenn hurried to the barn for halters and went to catch their horses. Lucy found herself alone with Bean. She had hoped to start work with the kids on her own, to find out how much they knew and to make a lesson plan.

"Bean, come show me the stable. Then we'll get a halter and catch Willy. You don't have to ride, but you do have to learn something today."

Still leaning on the paddock fence, Bean said, "See

Radar over there! He's the big horse chasing Willy. And the other one is Gulliver, Brett's new horse."

"Come on, Bean, don't try to distract me. Lead the way."

Nevertheless, as they headed for the stable, Lucy turned to look at Radar. The big bay was a powerful animal, with a commanding head and muscular body. All four feet were marked with white socks.

At the stable door Bean picked up an old soccer ball and tossed it out to the paddock. "It's Willy's. Willy plays soccer. He rings doorbells too."

"I'll have to see that!"

Lucy studied the stable—basically a center aisle with sliding doors at each end. To her right was an orderly tack room, on the left a large feed bin almost as tall as Bean. Together they walked past the roomy box stalls, five on one side, four on the other.

"That last one's not a stall," Bean said. "It's got a drain so you can wash a horse inside. Susannah built it for Toy, but everyone can use it."

What a luxury on a broiling hot day! Opposite the wash stall was a utility room for wheelbarrows, pitchforks, and other equipment. The whole setup was terrific.

Lucy took a small halter from the pony's stall and handed it to Bean.

"Willy's hard to catch," he said, inspecting the leather. "I've watched."

"Then go back to the feed bin, find a small bucket, and bring along a handful of oats."

Bean's face brightened. "That's a good idea. Willy's a pig. He's always eating."

Behind them Kit and Glenn brought their horses inside to the crossties. Bean scampered off to the feed bin and Lucy laughed to see him hang over the edge so that he was almost falling in.

When they went out into the paddock together, Bean said, "Do you know why Willy's mane and tail are that light color?"

"You mean flaxen?"

"Yeah. Well, when he was dipped in chocolate, that's how they were holding him." He raised his skinny arms as though lifting the horse in the air.

"You've got a good imagination, Bean. I think that's just what happened," Lucy said.

By the time they'd caught Willy, Kit and Glenn were riding their horses with Susannah as instructor. At first Lucy watched from the stable aisle while she showed Bean how to use a curry comb and brush. When they'd turned the pony loose, she focused on the kids in the ring. Though enthusiastic and unafraid, they were sloppy riders with no polish at all. For today she'd have to stand back and say nothing. But that was just as well, since her mind was full of the big bay horse with the four white socks.

The minute Susannah left for the yacht club with Kit and Glenn, Lucy caught Radar. She groomed him quickly and brought him to the ring. Bean watched from the fence as they spent fifteen minutes working "on the flat" at a walk, trot, and canter. Lucy's happiness grew with each turn of the ring. Radar was all the horse she needed and more. He was athletic and responsive; he was beautifully trained.

Suddenly a car motor roared nearby. Lucy tightened

her legs on the saddle in case Radar spooked. A red sports car pulled up, the car door slammed, and a short young man marched toward the ring.

"What the devil are you doing on my horse? Where do you come off even to get *near* my horse?"

"Brett, it's *Lucy*," Bean said from the fence. "The one who's helping with us kids and the horses."

"I don't care *who* she is." Brett vaulted the ring rail. "Get off my horse or I'll pull you off!"

Chapter Three

Lucy stared at the slight, brown-haired young man striding toward her, fists on his hips and dark eyes blazing. She sat tall in the saddle and tried to look tough.

"Hold it," she said. "Your uncle told me I could ride this horse. It was part of our agreement. I think you should talk to *him*!"

Brett stopped several steps in front of Radar. Lucy was surprised by his delicate face and slender body, nothing like the macho type she'd imagined.

"I'll do just that," Brett fumed. "But this is *my* horse and he's been my horse for the past nine years." His hostile expression suddenly gave way to a crooked smile. "On the other hand, it's not the first time Austin's made trouble thinking he runs the world. Where did he come off—"

"Look, I'm sorry about this. We can straighten it out when your uncle gets back tomorrow." She swallowed hard. "But I'm staying on this horse for the rest of my ride—another, uh, fifteen minutes. And if you want me off before then, you *will* have to pull me off."

Brett's answer was a defiant stare, but Lucy clenched her teeth and stared back. She had no idea how long their eyes locked, but after a while he strode back to his car and drove off.

"Don't worry," a small voice said from the fence behind Lucy. "What Uncle Austin says, goes."

For a moment Lucy was startled. She'd forgotten all about Bean. She walked Radar over to the fence. Was it right to ask an eight-year-old to talk about his uncle? Not really. Just the same, she found herself saying, "Bean, what did Brett mean about your uncle running the world? Is Uncle Austin unfair a lot of the time?"

"I'm having a fight with him right now, myself."

Lucy suppressed a laugh. The little guy was so serious. "What's up, Bean? Why?"

"About the horses. He broke his promise."

Lucy's stomach tightened. If Austin broke promises, Brett might win after all.

"What did he promise?"

"My mother said I didn't have to ride. No one has to like everything. I wouldn't have stayed here again if I had to ride. Then my mother goes to Japan and Uncle Austin changes everything. He says I've *got* to ride and he gets you to come and make sure."

Under the suntan Bean's face turned red with anger. "I might go on a huge hunger strike. I've been thinking it over. I might even run away."

"You know that's silly."

"I *could* run away. I'm thinking *that* over too."

The enormous eyes in that serious little face were hard to resist. And it did seem as though Austin had been unfair. "Bean, I'll make you a promise of my own," Lucy said, "and I keep my promises. I won't make you ride. I won't make you feel funny about it if you don't get up on a horse at all. But you'll have to learn *something* or I won't be doing my job. You'll have to help me around the barn the way you started to do today and you'll have to learn as much *about* horses as you can—the parts of the body, the bridle, the saddle . . ."

Beans eyes brightened. "That part's okay. I'm good at learning things."

"All right, then. I'll work out a plan. Now I'd better finish my ride."

As Lucy trotted Radar to the end of the ring, she wondered if she'd been foolish. It was wrong for Austin to break his promise to Bean. But wasn't she breaking her promise to *Austin*? And where did that leave their deal about Radar?

There just had to be a way to get Bean on a horse. She was sure that taking off the pressure was the way to start. And Mr. Kendrick would have some good ideas. She could phone him. But first she'd try to work it out by herself.

• • •

The afternoon sun beat down on the Mosedale dock as Allison walked out to where Lucy was sitting.

"Hi!" Lucy said happily, and went on rubbing sun block on her shoulders. "Keep me company. The sun's great."

"No letters. I'm sorry."

Lucy looked up at Allison. "I'll bet my letter with the Shelby Island address never got to Ken. When he left, I was going to be in Connecticut."

"Wait and see. You'll probably get a letter tomorrow. Where are the kids?"

"Glenn and Kit are at the yacht club with Susannah. Bean's swimming between the jetties." Lucy pointed to the small figure slithering through the water. "Watch him go. He's in training for some school team back home."

"Look, I can't stay, but we'll talk on the phone, okay?"

Lucy checked her watch. "Wait. I'll get Bean out of the water and go up with you. I'm supposed to meet with Susannah at three."

Bean padded along in front of them as they walked to the house. Though wrapped in a beach towel, his skinny body shivered all the way. There was no sign of Susannah in the living room, but someone was knocking on the front door. Through a pane of glass at the center Lucy saw an elderly man with a weathered face. "It's Amos," Allison said at her shoulder. "Let him in."

In the doorway Amos stared at Allison. "You don't look a bit like the kid who rode on my tractor all them years ago."

Allison smiled. "Guess not."

"How come you're visiting over here?"

"This is my friend, Lucy Hill. She's working for the Mosedales till the end of July."

"Pleased to meet you. You wouldn't be knowing if Miss Mosedale's home?"

"She'll be here any minute. Around three o'clock."

"Why, thanks. I'll be out in my truck by the garage."

"Did you see Mom's old car out there?" Allison said. "I'm allowed to drive it in the country."

"You sure *are* growed up!"

Lucy followed Allison and Amos outside. "Isn't that Ralph Ricosa's Jeep behind your truck?" Allison said with surprise.

"Ralph, the caretaker?" Lucy asked. "The one who was fired?"

Amos nodded. "He and Mr. Mosedale had quite a set-to last week. Ralph was telling me he's come for an electric drill he left over here. He was heading for the boathouse when I seen him last." Amos looked up the drive. "I've got to talk to Miss Mosedale right away."

"That's strange," Allison said, watching Amos go back to his truck. "Those old islanders are never in any kind of a hurry."

"He seemed pretty calm to me."

"Because you don't know the island. Anyway, he won't have long to wait."

The Mosedale station wagon turned into the end of the driveway. As Lucy and Allison met the car at the front door, Amos hovered nearby.

"Are you waiting for me, Amos?" Susannah asked.

"Sure am, Miss Mosedale. It's mighty important,"

"Of course, but aren't your questions best discussed with Mr. Mosedale? He'll be home tonight."

"It can't wait!" Amos looked back toward his truck. "Could you walk over there with me, Miss Mosedale?"

"Certainly." She spotted the Jeep. "Isn't that Ralph Ricosa's Jeep? He knows better than to come here!" She turned to Lucy. "I'll meet all of you in the house shortly."

Lucy walked Allison to her car, then went to the

house with Kit and Glenn. In the living room Bean came
running.

"Glenn, look! Ralph's down there. Wouldn't Uncle
Austin flip out?" Bean stretched his small body as tall as
it would go and tried to lower his voice. "How dare that
man come back on my property? I told him never to
show his face here again."

From the living-room window Lucy and the three
cousins watched a muscular, dark-haired man of about
thirty as he walked up the path from the dock. No one
moved until his blue-striped shirt disappeared around
the kitchen end of the house.

Lucy sat down on a bench in the living room. It was
an extraordinary room, two stories high, topped by a
cathedral ceiling and all of knotty pine. A massive stone
fireplace, easily six feet wide, gaped from one end. High
above the mantel a huge moose head stared down from
the wall. Lucy felt uncomfortable every time she saw it.
How would old Bull Moose Mosedale have liked to end
up on a wall?

Several minutes later Susannah walked into the
house. Lucy stood up, but Susannah walked through the
room without even a look in their direction. She hurried
to the "telephone closet" near the bedroom wing. Lucy
heard, "Haddem, it's extremely important that I see you
right away." The closet door closed on the rest of her
words.

• • •

"We'll be eating out on the porch until the renova-
tion's finished," Susannah said as she led Lucy and the

cousins to dinner that night. To Lucy's surprise Brett looked up from the table and got to his feet.

"Hello, Susannah," he said, holding his aunt's chair.

Lucy tried to hide her confusion at his polite manners and his charming grin. Could this be the same obnoxious guy she'd met that afternoon?

As Susannah took her chair, she reached up and patted Brett's face. "Good evening, Brett. I'm pleased you decided to join us." She looked toward Lucy. "I don't think you've met my nephew, Brett Mosedale. Brett, this is Lucy Hill, who's helping with the children and the horses for a few weeks."

"We've met, all right," Brett said as he returned to his chair. "And you and I have something to straighten out about that."

"Oh?" Susannah motioned Lucy to the seat next to Brett. "Shall we just enjoy our dinner and postpone any problems until later?" She looked toward the kitchen. "Margaret's made her famous leg of lamb, and there's fresh corn tonight too."

Lucy tried to ignore Brett close beside her. He's just a little runt, she said to herself. Spoiled and nasty. Just then Brett gave her that crooked smile she'd seen at the stable. His eyes had a mischievous look, as though hiding a special secret.

Margaret, the Irish housekeeper, brought a big platter of lamb and garden vegetables to the table. "Don't be bashful," Susannah urged Lucy. "Margaret's lamb has been the *specialité de la maison* since she and her husband came to work for us thirty years ago."

Lucy helped herself to two slices of lamb, but she was losing her appetite fast. Susannah was obviously very fond of Brett. According to Allison, Brett's parents had died when he was three; Susannah must have helped to bring him up. Would she give in to him about Radar?

"Come on, Susannah," Brett said, as soon as he'd helped himself to the lamb. "We're going to talk about this *now*. Did Austin promise Lucy my horse?"

This time Susannah answered immediately. "Your *Uncle* Austin made an arrangement—yes."

Lucy began to review the other horses in the barn. Toy and Gulliver were out, and, of course, the pony. Frisbee and Jonah would never be in shape to "show" if the kids were on their backs each day. It had to be Radar!

Her attention came back to the table as Susannah raised her voice. "Brett, I want this conversation to end. You'll have to accept what Austin decides, and that's all."

Brett nodded his head in a taunting bow. "Of course! Austin *always* decides because Austin controls the purse strings. Isn't that the way it goes?"

"Brett, I've asked you to stop!" For a moment Susannah's gray eyes pleaded. Then she looked away quickly and squared her shoulders. She turned back to the table with an appealing smile.

"I've some exciting news for you all—extraordinary news, which you'll find hard to believe. I wanted to wait until Uncle Austin came home, but—"

"Tell us."

"Come on, Aunt Suze."

"Believe it or not, it's about *treasure*. After all these years!"

Treasure? Lucy thought over the squeals of disbelief. When could Susannah have found a treasure? Come to think of it, she had certainly acted peculiar after speaking to Amos. She'd forgotten all about their three o'clock appointment to talk about managing the stable. Instead, Haddem had rushed across the harbor in his Boston Whaler. Lucy had seen him briefly—a tall man with a round face and a triangle of red hair growing down toward his forehead.

Susannah went on, "This afternoon, when we came home from sailing, Amos came to me with a small moldy box—"

"And it was full of money," Brett said skeptically.

"Was it the Old Judge's money?" Glenn asked.

"You're not making this up, Aunt Suze?"

Only Bean was silent, his big eyes staring.

"The box *was* filled with twenty-four gold coins, it really was—double eagles, Haddem calls them. He came over to see the coins this afternoon." She turned to Lucy. "Haddem is an old friend who edits a magazine on antiques. He knows a great deal about old coins."

"I've never seen any United States gold coins," Kit exclaimed.

"Of course not. They went out of circulation long before you were born—1933, Haddem reminded me. They're picked up by collectors now and·they're—"

"Where are the coins, Susannah? When can we see them?" Brett said.

"*Now*, Aunt Susannah, pl-ease!"

"Where did Amos find them?" Lucy asked.

"His men knocked out another section of the wine cellar this morning and the box tumbled to the ground. Those thick walls were a good hiding place."

"Why wouldn't he have used a metal box?" Glenn said.

Lucy answered, "He probably didn't expect the money to stay there long." Allison's father had said just last night that Judge Trabert must have been planning a getaway. This is crazy, Lucy thought. No loot turns up for more than half a century, and then the first day I'm here . . .

"Good thing it was Amos out there," Glenn said.

Kit glowered. "Don't be so suspicious. Just because *you*'d be tempted—"

"Anyone might be tempted," Susannah interrupted. "But you're right, Glenn. Amos can be trusted com—"

"Then where was the box all day?" Brett said. "Why didn't Amos give it to you when he found it?" Lucy glanced at Brett. She'd been wondering the same thing.

"You have to understand that Amos is an older person used to working for Austin and talking to 'the man of the house.' He was terribly excited when he found the box and not entirely sure what to do, so he sent the men to another job and locked the box in his truck. When he decided he should give to *me*, I'd already left for the yacht club."

"You still haven't told us when we'll see the coins," Brett said impatiently.

"Not until Haddem finishes checking on their value. Since his magazine deals with all kinds of antiques, he knows a number of experts on old coins."

"How long will that take?" Kit asked eagerly.

"I'm not sure. The condition of each coin is important and an accurate appraisal takes time. But they should be back in a few days."

"I could show you *my* double eagle," Bean said quietly, "if someone could help me get it from under the oats."

Glenn glowered at Bean. "Give me a break."

"No, no, it's true. I found it when I was hiding under the tarpaulin. I felt a coin in the dark and just put it in my pocket. But it must have been one of the gold coins—"

"What do you bet it's not?" Glenn said.

"That's enough, Glenn," Susannah said.

"I thought it was a half-a-dollar, but I haven't felt so many of those either. Up at the stable the coin fell into the feed bin. I tried to get it, but it just went down *more*. Please, Lucy. Come get it with me. We could take out all the oats and—"

"No, Bean," Susannah said. "It's been a long day for Lucy already and we're not going to dump all those oats."

Lucy studied Susannah's face. Was she just trying to save Bean from the disappointment of finding out his coin wasn't gold? Or did she suspect he hadn't found a coin at all?

Bean jumped up and ran to his aunt. Several raised red spots had appeared on his face. "I found a coin and I'm sure it's gold. No one believes me, but it's true."

How about *me*, Lucy asked herself. Do I believe him? If the box had tumbled open, a coin could have rolled into a corner where the workmen had missed it. But she'd already admired Bean's imagination.

"You'll all see twenty-four gold pieces soon enough," Susannah said evenly. "Bean, sit down now and have your dessert. Peach ice cream, I think."

Brett tipped his chair back. "Wait till Austin hears

about this one," he said with a short whistle. "Will this be a five-way split, do you think?"

"Of course," Susannah said quickly. "The money was found in the house."

"Old Austin'll find some way to hang on to mine, I'm sure. He's good at that." Brett put his napkin on the table. "May I be excused?"

"Definitely. You're not very good company tonight."

He walked around to Susannah and kissed her cheek. "Sorry, Aunt Suze."

Susannah patted his face affectionately, as she'd done when they first sat down. No wonder he was spoiled rotten, Lucy thought. He just turned on the charm. Charm? What was she saying? He wasn't charming at all!

Chapter Four

Lucy raised her head off the pillow. A spike of light escaped the side of the window shade and speared one eye. Confused, she reached for her clock. Had she slept through the alarm? No, the time read seven, not seven-fifteen. And what was that weird sound? It seemed impossible. A *trumpet*—at this hour! Lucy slipped on a robe and followed the sound to the hall window. Sure enough, there was Glenn standing beside the flagpole and pulling on the ropes. Nearby, a tall man in khaki Bermuda shorts and a light blue sport-shirt held a bugle to his mouth. His back was perfectly straight and his large craggy face absolutely serious. Austin Mosedale had come home.

Lucy hurried to wash and dress. Surely no one could have slept through that bugle, but maybe the kids would stay in their rooms. This was her first day in charge of the stable and she really wanted to go to the barn alone.

Lucy remembered Bean's coin as she walked along the path in the woods. Was there even the faintest chance that she'd find it in the feed bin this morning?

The stable was beautiful in the early light. Someday

she'd have a setup of her own like this—*just* like this, except that she'd paint the barn gray with white trim and use blue-checked blankets and sheets. For now, she could imagine this stable was hers. And she'd keep these horses more fit and better groomed than they'd ever been before!

The horses, too, seemed to have heard the morning bugle. Lucy laughed to see all six of them standing at attention behind their stall doors.

"Good morning, guys," she called, and hurried to the hayloft. "Don't worry. Breakfast's coming."

An hour later Lucy herself could hardly wait for breakfast. Feeding and mucking out in new surroundings had taken longer than she'd expected. Back at the house she hurried toward the porch. Mr. Mosedale's voice boomed from the table.

"You'll be racing every Sunday, Glenn?"

"I hope so. Haddem says Mr. Payne's a great sailor and I'll learn a lot."

Lucy walked onto the porch. "Good morning, Mr. Mosedale."

"Hi, Lucy," the kids said in unison.

"Good morning, everybody. Where's Bean?"

"Reading on the glider." Kit pointed to an old-fashioned porch couch that was moving back and forth on a metal frame.

Austin Mosedale finished his orange juice. "Good morning, Lucy Hill," he said. "Welcome to Shelby Island. How are you getting on?"

"Fine, thank you, Mr. Mosedale."

"She's great, Uncle Austin."

Lucy felt herself blush as she sat down. "Kit, I've been here just one—"

"Well, today's another," Austin said quickly. "Kit and Glenn ride rather well, don't you think?"

Fighting for time, Lucy helped herself to a bran muffin. "It's great to see how athletic they are," she said slowly. "I think we're going to accomplish a lot."

For the first time Mr. Mosedale looked at Lucy with interest. "A careful answer," he said. "Well, let's see what you can do with them. And Bean, too, of course."

"Of course."

Should she wait for Susannah or face Austin herself?

"I do need to ask you about Radar. I understood that I would be allowed to ride him; is that right? And to show him too?"

Austin rubbed his chin. "That's what we agreed. I came in very late last night, so Susannah and I haven't had a chance to talk. Are you having difficulty with the horse?"

"Not with the *horse*. With his owner."

Anger flashed across Austin's face. "You can leave that to me. Brett will have to be satisfied to work that new horse he insisted on buying. . . ." He forced his face into a more genial expression and pushed back his chair.

"We'll talk some more later today. I've a schedule to keep and I'm sure you do too." Tucking the morning paper under his arm, he left without waiting for an answer.

As Austin's words hovered over the table, Bean came over to a chair next to Lucy. At the same time Margaret appeared with a heaping platter of scrambled eggs and bacon.

"I guess Uncle Austin doesn't know about the coins yet," Glenn said. "If Aunt Susannah went to bed . . ."

"Probably not," Lucy said, "and I think we should all wait for Susannah to tell him. She'll get to it right away, I'm sure."

Lucy ate her eggs eagerly and thought about Austin. He'd been nice enough to *her*. . . .

"Lucy, *do* we have a schedule?" Kit asked suddenly.

"Well, I've been working on it. You and Glenn have sailing and tennis in the afternoons. If we're going to ride in the morning, it would feel great to have a swim before lunch. That means we should get to the barn by nine. We'll groom and then ride until eleven."

"When will *you* ride? We want to see you ride," Kit said. But she was looking away from the table as she spoke, watching Austin walk into the boathouse.

"I'll ride around four o'clock, I think. And maybe again after supper. We'll see. The important thing is to get the two of you going. You'll have to be patient while I find out how much you already know. How long have you been riding?"

"The summers we've been here."

"That's three," Glenn said. But he, too, looked over at the boathouse.

"Has Susannah been your only teacher?"

Kit nodded.

"Sometimes Brett told us a few things," Glenn said. "Say, Lucy, may I be excused?"

Lucy was startled. It was strange to be the person you asked for permission to leave. "Well—what's the problem, Glenn?"

"There's something wrong. Uncle Austin should be

getting into his rowboat by now. You can clock his routine."

"You want to check on him?"

Glenn was already at the porch door. "Yeah!"

"Glenn's right," Kit said. "First, Uncle Austin goes to the boathouse for his life jacket. Then he walks back to the beach for his rowboat."

"He can't swim, you know," Bean said, with a note of satisfaction. "He's really scared of the water."

By now Glenn had disappeared from sight. No one spoke while they waited for him to reappear.

"I'm going down there," Kit said. Lucy and Bean got up from the table, too, and all three of them hurried across the patio. As they headed for the beach, Glenn ran up the dock.

"Get Susannah," he shouted. "Tell her to call the volunteer ambulance."

Kit and Bean sped toward him.

"What happened?"

"Is he okay?"

"I'm not sure. The big wooden locker fell on top of him. He's breathing all right, but he's out cold."

• • •

"Where will they take him?" Lucy asked. No one had moved out of range of the phone since the ambulance left. "There can't be a hospital on this tiny island!"

"They'll take the ferry to Greenpoint," Glenn said. "Susannah took *me* to that hospital, too, the time I broke my arm."

"How heavy do you think that locker is?"

"*Plenty* heavy—even empty. And then all Uncle Austin's fishing gear is in there—the stuff he uses himself and for guests on the *Gismo*. And extra life jackets. Once in a while there's the extra motor for Brett's boat—when he bothers to put it away."

"He didn't this time. I saw it on the floorboards yesterday," Kit said.

"I guess that was a good thing. It's a heavy motor."

"Hello! What's going on?" A stocky young man with sideburns and a beard was crossing the patio. He held a basket of strawberries.

Bean waved hello. "Mr. Beech must have heard the siren."

"What's going on?" Mr. Beech asked again, opening the door to the porch. "I was out picking berries. It never occurred to me the ambulance was coming here. Then I saw the men with the stretcher walking up the dock." He was suddenly aware of Lucy. "Sorry, I'm Ed Beech. I rent the McCauleys' guesthouse for the month of July." He waved toward a small white house with red shutters on the other side of the plum trees.

"He's a science teacher in a high school in Pennsylvania," Bean said. "I learn from him lots."

"Exactly what happened to Austin?" Ed Beech said.

"You know the big locker in the boathouse? It came down on top of him. He was just laying there flat on his back."

Lucy heard her mother's voice in her ear: "Lying, not laying." She decided to keep quiet. She hadn't been hired to teach grammar.

"That's terrible, Glenn," Mr. Beech was saying. "Did he know what happened?"

"He was out cold when I found him. I think it was

from hitting the back of his head on the floorboards. It looked as though he'd been moving out of the way, because the locker was on top of his side."

Lucy looked up at Beech. "He was talking by the time the ambulance came, though he was pretty dazed."

"Yeah," Glenn went on. "He was cursing and trying to figure out what happened."

Bean did his Austin imitation: "How the H could that blankety-blank cupboard come loose from the wall?"

"I don't feel much like riding today," Glenn said. "I'd like to stick around until we hear everything's okay."

"I—I'd like to ride," Kit said, "but it doesn't seem right. Uncle Austin could be hurt real bad."

Ed smiled at them. "Don't worry. It sounds as though he got lucky. I'm going to take these strawberries to Margaret; they're even juicier than last year. Then you can all come back to my dock and we'll find specimens for the saltwater aquarium I've started. Margaret will phone us when she gets some news."

After a short debate Lucy and the kids followed Ed to the kitchen. They found Margaret with red eyes, muttering about "poor Mr. Austin" and "that no-account Ralph."

"Isn't it something awful," she said, accepting the strawberries. "Ralph never was one to keep after things. My husband Mitchell's always been telling me that."

There were footsteps at the back porch. "Well, and will you look who's coming through the door now," Margaret said, putting the berries into the refrigerator. "And didn't you go sleeping through everything that's happened."

Brett walked into the kitchen. "What's all the excitement about?" He sidled up to Margaret with an impish smile and gave her a big hug. "You're not going to be cross with me now, are ye?" His brogue imitated hers perfectly.

"Now get on with you. I suppose you'll be wanting breakfast at this hour. Your uncle's had a serious accident. He's gone off in the ambulance, that's what's happened, and you sleeping right through it all like a dead one."

"What? What kind of an accident?"

"The locker in the boathouse fell on top of him, and he's surely broken some bones," Glenn said. "Aunt Susannah went off with him and we're waiting to hear."

For a moment Brett looked concerned. Then he turned to Lucy as though he'd just realized she was there. "I guess you didn't have a chance to ask about Radar. So I hope you won't ride him until Austin gets back."

"I did talk to Austin, Brett—at breakfast this morning. He said he'd promised me the horse for the month of July and to leave the problem to him. I'm sorry, but it's only about three and a half weeks."

"A horse can be ruined in a tenth that time."

"I know, but I respect what you've done with Radar and I'm an experienced rider. Why not come up and watch me ride him?" She forced herself a step farther. "You can give me some advice."

Brett started for the door. "Mags, never mind breakfast. I'll drive down to Dahl's." Before he walked out, he turned to Lucy. "Thanks, but no thanks. You can just struggle with the horse by yourself."

• • •

"Can you come over for a while?" Allison said that night on the phone.

"I'm too tired, Allison. These two days feel like twenty."

"Any mail for you today?"

"No. And it's been a crazy day over here."

"What was the final word on Austin?"

"Two cracked ribs and a badly sprained ankle. He twisted the ankle getting out of the way. Then the edge of the locker broke the ribs. I guess he was lucky."

"He sure was lucky. I know that locker. If it had cracked his head . . ."

Lucy remembered about the gold coins. When Susannah came back from the hospital she'd warned them all to say nothing. She wasn't going to speak to Austin until he felt better. But what a tough secret to keep from Allison!

"How are you making out with the kids?" Allison asked.

"The real ones or the 'enfant terrible'?"

"You've met Brett, then?"

"Unfortunately."

"Come on, Lucy. He's a scary guy when he's drinking and he can fly off the handle when you least expect it, but you have to admit he's got charm."

"Not for me, he hasn't. Anyway, Kit and Glenn are really good kids, but I can see that they're bored with riding. Susannah won't let them jump, did I tell you? I guess because she's never ridden anything but Saddlebreds, she thinks jumping is dangerous. Both kids have lots to learn on the flat, but they'd have to *care*. I've got to think of a way to get them involved."

"And Bean?"

"I'm crazy about him, but he's a stubborn little guy." Lucy sighed. "Look, I don't want to think about any of them anymore. I'm going to walk outside and get away from all the Mosedales and their yards of knotty pine. Then I'll hit the sack."

"Okay. Talk soon."

"You bet."

Lucy walked up to the barn and checked on the horses. The stars were spectacular in a clear moonlit sky. She traced the big dipper and searched for Orion. Ed Beech had a big telescope in front of his house. Maybe he could help her find it.

It was hard to be away from Ken on a night like this. Eleven days had gone by since they'd talked, eleven days without even a letter. She kicked the driveway, sending up a shower of pebbles.

On the harbor side of the house Lucy replayed the morning—Glenn running up the dock and shouting for help, Austin lying on the stretcher, too tall for a comfortable fit. What was Austin really like? So far it was hard to tell, but he certainly wasn't the most popular man around!

A small shiver stopped Lucy where she stood. She'd like to have another look at that locker. Perhaps she'd just been caught up in too many mysteries in the past, but why had that locker come loose from the wall?

Walking down the dock, Lucy wondered if she should

go back to the stable for a flashlight. Then she realized that the boathouse windows all faced away from the house. She could probably put on the overhead light without being seen.

The tall wooden locker was standing against the wall where the ambulance men had replaced it after freeing Austin. Lucy found a metal ladder and opened it carefully. She climbed up until she could see the angle irons screwed into the top of the locker. Then she studied the spots where they'd been attached to the wall.

Lucy's heart began to race. The holes in the wall looked too clean. Not one was enlarged and there was no sign of splintering. Those screws hadn't pulled loose. Someone had deliberately removed them.

Lucy climbed down the ladder and walked up to the locker, pretending to be Austin. How come nothing had fallen out of the cabinet when it fell forward? She checked the latch at the bottom of the door. Then she saw the nail. Someone had nailed the bottom of the door to the base of the cabinet. In fact, the center of the door was nailed shut too.

So much for Austin's accident. When he'd reached the locker that morning, he'd found the door stuck. He'd probably tugged at it hard. Detached from the wall, the whole locker had pitched forward.

Shouldn't she tell someone about this? Ralph, who'd quarreled with Austin, had been in the boathouse just yesterday. Probably Brett had been there too. Did anyone else have it in for Austin?

Lucy sat down at the end of the dock and stared into the dark water. She had all kinds of new people to get along with, six horses to look after, and three kids to teach riding—one of whom refused even to get up on a pony. Lucy, she asked herself, do you need to solve a mystery too?

Chapter Five

"Come on, Gulliver, move over." Lucy gave Brett's young jumper a swat on the rump to move him away from the wheelbarrow. "What a beautiful animal you are. I see why Brett was so set on buying you."

Lucy pushed the wheelbarrow outside to the manure pile and wondered why Brett wasn't looking after his own horse. Because he's spoiled, she answered herself. But that's none of your business. You're being paid to take care of six horses and if one of them's Brett's, that's that.

The morning stable routine was easier the second time around, and it was reassuring to be doing the old familiar things she'd done so often in the past. She'd just given the horses their grain when she heard her name called softly from the top of the aisle.

"Loo-cee."

"Hi! Who's there? Kit? Bean?"

"It's me." Bean walked between the stalls, checking the whereabouts of each horse he passed. "I came to help you feed the oats."

"That's great, Bean. But I feed the horses first thing so they'll have time to digest their breakfast before we ride. You can help at noon, if you like."

"Sure, Lucy." He continued to look up at her without moving.

"What is it, Bean?"

"There really was a coin. And I'm pretty sure it was gold. Do you believe me?"

Lucy looked away. Faced with those huge gray eyes, it was hard to answer truthfully. She rested the pitchfork against the wall. "Come to the tack room with me, okay?"

It was possible that Bean had found some kind of a coin. Why not? Anyone from Austin or a workman could have dropped a coin in the wine cellar.

"Tell me how you found the coin."

"I was crawling around and my fingers touched something hard. It was too flat and slippery to be a stone. You were calling me then so I just picked it up and dropped it into my pocket. I told you last night, I thought it was half-a-dollar. Anyway, I was mostly thinking about horses and how to keep off them."

"But now you've decided it was gold. Why is that?"

"Well, we heard about the box. It could have tumbled out. Anyway, I just know it."

"Do you also know what people think when you talk like that? They think you've made all this up to get attention, to be part of an exciting story. After all, finding treasure *is* exciting."

Bean just stared ahead.

"Do you understand what I'm saying?"

Finally Bean nodded. He said in a small voice, "I don't care what anyone thinks but you."

Lucy studied him. What a sweet kid! There must have been some kind of a coin, she thought. Bean had shown up to feed the horses. There could be no other reason but to get into the oats. With Bean on the job she'd better watch out. The horses would be getting double rations!

To show faith in his story would definitely be to her advantage. Winning Bean's affection was her best hope for getting him on a horse. Was it right, though, to get your way by lying to a child? What about a white lie?

"I believe you, Bean. I believe you found a coin and that you're sure it's gold. When we get farther down into the oats we'll see."

A tiny smile wriggled onto his cheeks. She'd hedged on the gold, but it seemed as though he hadn't noticed. Lucy put an arm around his shoulders. "Have you ever seen a frog on a pony?"

Bean looked at her quizzically. "I've seen a *dog* on a pony. In the circus."

"Well, come with me and I'll show you right now."

Lucy walked over to Willy in the paddock with Bean following behind. She lifted the pony's front leg and pointed to a rubbery triangular pad at the back of the foot. "This is the horse's main shock absorber and it's called the 'frog.'"

Bean was grinning from ear to ear. "Say, Lucy, that's great. Wait till I try it on Kit—but I'll say four frogs. Willy's got four feet."

"You do that. Now let's get some breakfast."

Bean ran ahead and Lucy felt sure he was already

planning what he'd say to Kit. She remembered that he'd
bent over Willy's foot with no trace of fear at all. If fear
wasn't his problem about riding, what *was*?

• • •

The porch glider squeaked up and down the scale as
Lucy rocked back and forth on the old metal frame. The
cousins had gone off clamming with Brett. To Lucy's
surprise he'd appeared at lunch to invite them all—even
her. She'd chosen to stay home and had just written
letters to her father in California and her mother in
Austria. Now she was trying to make a lesson plan.

That morning, after breakfast, she'd finally had a
chance to teach Kit and Glenn by herself. As she'd sus-
pected, they had little interest in improving their riding
and no idea of what that would mean. They trusted their
horses. They liked to go out on the trail. And even in the
ring, they enjoyed the exercise. But that was about all.
Lucy was determined to teach them *something* more so
she wouldn't feel that she'd cheated the Mosedales. But
how much could she accomplish in three weeks? And
how could she make them understand that riding was a
highly skilled sport like tennis or sailing? The more you
knew, the more fun it could be.

The air was heavy and the harbor had turned silver
under a hazy sky. Even in shorts and a thin shirt Lucy was
uncomfortably warm. The vinyl cushions stuck to the
back of her bare legs. The lulling motion of the glider
made her eyes droop. A few minutes later she fell asleep.

Suddenly Austin's voice reverberated from the living-room window: "I don't see how you could have been

so foolish, Susannah. Haddem's not to be trusted with money. You know that very well."

Lucy scrunched down lower in the glider. Should she get up right now and walk away? But if she did, wouldn't they wonder how long she'd been listening?

"All right, Austin, we all know Haddem's problem, but he's the one who suffers, not his friends. With the stakes he plays for, our few twenty-dollar gold pieces aren't at risk."

"It all depends how much he's lost this year, doesn't it?"

"Haddem wouldn't cheat his friends. Aren't you being unfair? You're not going back to that poker game at college—not after all these years?"

"I never had proof that he cheated and I never said that I did. I just know that he was desperate at the time. He'd managed to go through a year's school allowance by January. Haddem and I played with the same guys every week and it was the only time in four years that everyone lost but Haddem—lost heavily. We all knew he cheated! If you remember, I didn't dare tell Father how much money Haddem took from me, even though it meant working weekends for months. . . ."

By now Lucy was too fascinated to leave if she could. But what would she do if Austin or Susannah walked over to the window and saw her there? Or if the kids came home and ran out onto the porch calling her name?

Susannah's voice was crisp. "Well, you had him thrown out of the fraternity after the game. You voted against his membership in the Shelby Golf Club. I'd say you evened the score! And don't you think it's time to forget this grudge?"

"Not that again, Susannah. No matter what Haddem thinks, I had nothing to do with the fraternity vote or the one at the club. Haddem *was* my friend and he's *still* my friend. Why, he plays bridge here every Wednesday night! But people with a habit they can't control remain a question mark. Haddem's a compulsive gambler, and if he were desperate again—I don't know. . . ." Austin paused. "In any case, Susannah, you should have waited until I came home. You had no right to act on your own."

"Didn't I? At least twice a summer I have to remind you that this house belongs to all of us—to me as much as to you. Those coins were found here. What gives you the right to make every decision by yourself?"

"Perhaps because I pay most of the bills."

Susannah surely loved that, Lucy thought. For a time there was silence on the other side of the window.

Finally, Susannah said, "You *will* admit that Haddem knows just about everything about antiques and collectibles—that what he doesn't know, he can find out from the best?"

"Yes, of course."

"And I did ask him for a receipt."

"You actually have a receipt?"

"Yes, dear brother, I'm not as foolish as you think!"

Susannah must have produced the receipt for Austin to read.

"There were twenty-four double eagles?" Lucy could sense Austin's excitement despite his even delivery.

"The dates are there too."

"Yes, I see. They were all from the two years—1926 and '27."

"Haddem says the judge probably picked up rolls of new coins from whatever bank he was near. He died in 1928."

The front door opened, followed by a torrent of chatter from the cousins. Lucy closed her eyes and tried to breath evenly, as if she were asleep, until she was certain the kids had gone off toward the kitchen.

"And when did Haddem think he'd bring the coins back?" Austin said when they'd left.

"In a few days. The condition of the coins affects their value, so he needed the particular twenty-dollar gold pieces for an accurate appraisal." Susannah's voice grew softer. They seemed to be leaving the room.

Lucy jumped up and walked around the back of the house toward the kitchen. It may have been wrong to eavesdrop, but perhaps she'd found another suspect for the "accident" in the boathouse. Clearly Haddem was another person with grievances against Austin. And he'd come across the bay to see Susannah—he'd tied up his Boston Whaler at the boathouse—just the afternoon before Austin came home.

● ● ●

That night Allison switched on the car radio as they drove along the quiet island road in the moonlight. "I'm going to show you the historic spot where Allison Barker had her first date."

"Great, Allison."

Lucy knew she was being especially quiet, but she couldn't seem to hook into Allison's mood.

"What's the matter, Lucy?" Allison said after a while. "Do you hate it over there?"

"I like the job better each day. But I'm worried about something and I need your advice. Last night, after we talked on the phone, I took another look at the locker that fell over on Austin. Allison, believe me, that 'accident' didn't just happen."

"Lucy! You're just looking for another mystery to solve. It's too tame for you on Shelby Island."

"No, Allison. I looked everything over carefully. There had been two large angle irons holding the locker to the wall. The holes were absolutely clean, the way they look when you take out the screws with a screwdriver."

"Were there any screws around?"

"Sure. Lying on the floor. But someone would have to be pretty dumb to plan an accident and walk off with the screws. Besides, there was something else. The door was nailed shut to make sure Austin would pull it extra hard and that the weight of the things in the cupboard would help to pitch it forward."

"Austin would have seen the nails."

"No, not the way they were put in at the very top and bottom. Not unless he was looking. Believe me, Allison." For a moment she felt like Bean with his coin. "Someone engineered that accident. My problem is what to do about it. Shouldn't Austin be told?"

"Of course he should. But are you the one to tell him?"

"That's really my point. How can I—almost a total stranger—say, even to Susannah, 'Someone is trying to hurt your brother'? Even if they looked at the locker again and agreed with me, they'd wonder why I was snooping around there. What business is it of mine anyway? And would they want me to know that someone hated Austin enough to do this? It might be embarrass-ing.''

"Well, you've answered yourself."

"I know, but I feel weird about it, Allison. Austin may be in serious danger."

Allison frowned. "Look at it this way. When his ankle's better, he'll get back to that locker and he'll see the nails for himself."

"Suppose something else happens in the meantime?"

"If you're right about this, and it's hard to believe, someone *may* try again even if Austin knows he's a target."

"Why is it so hard to believe? Lots of people seem to dislike the man."

"Enough to injure him seriously?"

"Possibly. The day before the accident that caretaker he fired, Ralph, was down at the boathouse supposedly looking for some tool he'd left behind. I saw him myself."

"You may have something there. Everyone on the island knows Ralph's got a temper to match Austin's."

"And how about Brett? He's plenty hot tempered. He might have wanted to get even with Austin for letting me ride Radar—that and a lot of other grievances. He could have gotten to the boathouse anytime. In fact anyone could. Haddem brought his boat across the day before." Lucy paused. "What goes on between Haddem and Austin, anyway?"

"I told you, they've known each other since college."

"Look, I don't mean to be a snoop. It's just—"

"It's just that you are one. I mean . . . you *are*, Lucy,

and you've helped a lot of people with the mysteries you've solved. It's okay if you know when to quit."

Allison turned the car into a small driveway and put on the brake. "Well, we're here. The Shelby Island Miniature Golf Course."

Lucy started to laugh. "Do you mean it? You really had your first date here? How old were you?"

"About ten!" Allison turned off the motor. "Where was your first date? At a horse show, I suppose."

Lucy blushed. "I guess it was, if you're counting from age ten. Ricky Harris bought me a can of soda too."

"Do I dare ask the daily question? Any mail?"

"*No* mail . . . and it's beginning to get me down. After all, how long does it take to write a few lines?"

"You thought Ken might not have your address."

"I know, but I'm through giving him the benefit of the doubt. I'm tired of waiting for a letter. I'm going to concentrate on the Mosedales and forget all about him. He's—"

"Give me a break! But seriously, Lucy, be careful about the Mosedales. They can be a lot of fun, particularly when Jane is around, but there's a lot of pride there too. They can go at each other, but the first hint of criticism from the outside and they'll gang up together—"

"Tell me about Haddem. I gather he has a special problem."

"He's a great antiquarian and makes plenty of money. But he's a compulsive gambler and loses in casinos around the world. I heard Dad say things were tight for him *now*, as a matter of fact. So far he's managed to hang on to his apartment in New York, but the Shelby house is his joy and Dad says he could lose it."

"Do you have any idea why he was kept out of the country club out here?"

"No. But people either love Haddem or hate him. He has this I-came-over-in-the-*Mayflower* manner and some people think he's arrogant."

"He seems to be a special friend of Susannah's."

"That goes back a long way. Susannah's rather handsome now, but with her big body and her long nose, she wasn't so great in her teens. We've got pictures at the house of all of them together, and you can see. Dad says Haddem was very decent about being Susannah's date—for special parties or the theater, whatever. I guess they stayed friends."

Allison's hand was on the door handle. "Come on. Let's tee off."

"Just one thing more. *Please,* Allison. Why would belonging to the country club be important to Haddem?"

"I suppose because Haddem expects to be welcome everywhere. I don't really know. The club is small, with a simple clubhouse, but I guess it means something to a lot of people here—especially if they like to golf. There's no public course on the island, remember."

"Except this one," Lucy said, laughing. "Let's play."

They paid their money and collected balls and putters. "Thanks for all the talk," Lucy said as she teed up in front of a small windmill.

"Anytime. But take my advice, Lucy. Just have fun over there and teach the kids how to ride. Don't dig around too much. You might turn up something that no one wants to see."

Chapter Six

Monday morning Lucy sat on the sand watching Kit hunt for a collection of scallop shells that would nest one inside the other. "Here, Kit," she said, spotting a shell no bigger than the half-moon on her thumb. "Have you got one this tiny?"

Kit claimed the shell and Lucy walked to the edge of the water. "Bean! Can you hear me? You'd better come out now or you'll dissolve."

The little figure turned toward shore, and Lucy smiled to herself as she went back up the beach. She was beginning to like it here. The Mosedales had made her welcome. The kids were fun and accepted her authority. Radar was the most exciting horse she'd ever ridden. The two of them seemed to communicate by ESP as well as through her legs and hands.

After the excitement of the first three days the relaxed weekend had been a pleasure. Though Austin was hobbling on a cane and wearing a chest brace, he and Susannah had been busy with houseguests. Glenn had raced at the yacht club each day. There had been time for a trail ride through the woods with Kit. And with Bean she'd helped Ed Beech attach an air pump to the saltwater aquarium he'd started the morning of the accident. They'd also moved the whole thing out of the sun. As of now, only the hermit crabs were staying alive.

Lucy still felt uncomfortable about Austin's "accident," but he would get to the boathouse soon and would probably draw his own conclusions.

Bean still hadn't been on a horse, but he was speeding up and down the stable aisles filling the feed tubs confidently. Yesterday he'd caught Willy without help and pulled the joke on Kit about the pony and the frog. Unfortunately, Kit had known that the "frog" was part of a horse's foot. But she'd encouraged Bean to try again with Glenn.

Brett, thank goodness, had stayed out of the way completely.

"Lucy! Bring everyone up to the house," Susannah called from behind the tiger lilies. "We're going off island."

Lucy stood up and brushed the sand off her legs. "We'll be right there."

"Isn't this a splendid idea?" Susannah said as she drove Lucy and the kids toward the South Ferry half an hour later. "Since the horses rest on Monday, we're not interfering with anyone's time at the barn. I promised Lucy she could 'show' Radar while she was here, and the show at Appentuck Farm two weeks from now seems the best choice. We'll pick up the prize list over there before lunch. Then we'll go on to Godsey's so Lucy can taste the best lobsters on the island. After lunch we'll have an ocean swim at Pam Firestone's. You'll enjoy the surf,

Lucy, after our calm harbor." Susannah took a deep breath. She seemed under some sort of strain.

This entire excursion seems to be planned around me, Lucy thought. What a nice thing for Susannah to do. Then why do I feel there's more to it than that?

"Wait till you see those lobsters," Glenn said.

"Do you like the ocean?" Kit asked.

"It all sounds great," Lucy said. "And we've lucked out on the weather too." The bright blue sky was streaked with trails of white. It looked as though some giant had been fingerpainting up there.

The big station wagon pulled behind the line of cars waiting for the South Ferry. The tubby white vessel was churning its way toward them slowly. Lucy could see that the bay was narrower on this side of the island than the other and the opposite shore quite built up.

"Can I get out, Aunt Susannah?" Bean asked.

"If you come back the second I blow the horn."

Lucy followed Bean toward the fence at the ferry slip. An old green Jeep was first in the car line.

"There's Ralph," Bean shouted. "Hello, Ralph."

"Hello there, Bean. How's it going?"

"Okay, Ralph." He ducked his head a minute, looking at Lucy. "I'm still holding out."

"That a boy, Bean. You stick to your guns."

Bean craned his neck to see into the back of the truck. "Where ya going with all that stuff? I thought you worked on Shelby Island."

"Not anymore, I don't. My brother's fixed me up with a family in Newport. I bet you don't know where that is."

"Newport, Rhode Island?"

"You always were a smart kid."

"Because of what Uncle Austin said?"

Ralph's face flushed. "You didn't believe that rubbish, did you?"

Bean shrugged his shoulders and looked uncertain.

"Your uncle couldn't keep me from working on the island, nohow. He doesn't own the place, whatever he thinks. I'm going to Newport because my brother's there and I'm going to make twice the money I can make around here." He looked toward the ferry. "You'd better get back in the car, Bean. You don't want to be left on shore."

Susannah's horn had started to beep. "Yeah," Bean said, twisting one leg around the other. "Yeah, Ralph. Well, so long."

Lucy put a hand behind Bean's back and urged him away gently. He dragged his feet a few moments, then raced off.

"Guess who we saw," he announced at the door of the station wagon. "Ralph's there in his Jeep and he's leaving for Newport."

"Are you sure?" Susannah said anxiously, as though it was a matter of great importance. She looked at Lucy for confirmation.

"That's what he said, Susannah, and from the amount of equipment in the Jeep he must be going *some-where*."

The ferryman waved them forward to the front of a new line so that their car ended up next to Ralph's Jeep. Every so often Ralph looked over at Susannah, but she turned away each time.

Kit said, "Aren't you even going to talk to him, Aunt Suze?"

"Absolutely not."

"But you told us Uncle Austin lost his temper and Ralph was the best caretaker you'd had in years."

"I did say that, I know. But—but I have more information now."

They know! Lucy thought. Austin's seen the nails in the locker door and they blame Ralph. *No*, wait a minute. Susannah blames Ralph, but I'll bet Austin is just as likely to blame Brett, as always. She took a deep breath. At least they *knew*.

Ralph was definitely her own first choice. She hoped she was right, since nothing could be proved and at least he was leaving the island. . . .

"Lucy, are you excited about the horse show?" Kit asked. "Can we all come and watch?"

"Of course!" Lucy said. "If someone will drive you over."

"I'll bring the children," Susannah said. "We'll all enjoy the day."

"How will Radar get there?" Glenn asked. "No one but Brett drives the trailer, and he hardly talks to Lucy."

Leave it to Glenn to come right out with it, Lucy thought as she shifted in her seat uncomfortably.

"Something will work out," Susannah said distractedly. Ralph was sliding across the front seat of the Jeep to the window.

"Hello, Miss Mosedale, did the kids tell you about my new job? I'm all fixed up in Newport, Rhode Island."

"Really?" Susannah said. Her voice was frosty.

"Come on, Miss Mosedale, you and me always got along. I thought you'd be glad for me."

"I am glad, Ralph. I'm glad you're leaving Shelby Island so we can enjoy the rest of the summer."

Ralph turned away quickly. Then he stepped out of his Jeep and walked to the front of the ferry. Lucy was startled. He'd looked as though he'd been slapped in the face. No one spoke in the car until they'd left the ferry and were well on their way to Sag Harbor.

• • •

Appentuck Farm was a beautiful spread of paddocks and fields, though, unlike Connecticut, the land was perfectly flat. Lucy imagined the striped canvas in place for the show and wished they were calling her class right then. As she picked up a prize list from a young girl in the office, an older woman with short black hair walked in and looked at her closely. "Don't I know you?" she said.

Lucy was puzzled. She searched her memory but couldn't place the woman at all.

"Aren't you one of John Kendrick's kids? I thought I saw you riding with him last summer at Eastchester."

Lucy broke into her widest smile. "You really remember?"

"John and I are good friends, though we seldom catch up with each other. Are we going to have you with us on the twenty-third? I didn't know Up and Down Farm came out this way."

"Mr. Kendrick won't be here, but I'm working this month on Shelby Island and the people I'm with are lending me a horse. It will be a strange feeling to be showing on my own."

"Will you be riding in the Maclay class?"

"No, Mr. Kendrick wants me to make it into Open first. I need one more blue ribbon 'Over Fences.'"

"Well, let me know if I can help in any way. Any kid of John's has a leg up with me." She put out her hand. "I'm Carola Tompkins and you're . . . Lucy . . ."

The woman even remembered her name! "Lucy Hill, Miss Tompkins. It's great to meet you, and thanks!"

Lucy walked back to the car in a daze. Suddenly the trip for lobsters seemed a waste of time. She even resented the Monday layoff for the horses. All she wanted to do was get back to the barn and work. From the time she'd been ten, riding and Mr. Kendrick had been one of the most reliable things in her life. Even more than her parents in some ways. Nothing—not even Ken and whatever he was up to in London—was going to get in the way. She'd even make friends with Brett, if that's what it took to get Radar to Appentuck!

Bean stuck his head out of the car window. "Lucy, you look so—sort of angry. What's the matter?"

"I'm not angry, Bean, just determined."

Lucy got back into the station wagon. "Thanks, Susannah. I really appreciate your taking the time to bring me here."

"You're most welcome, Lucy. And *now* for lobsters!"

Lucy began to study the prize list. When she finally looked up, the cousins were involved in a car game and Susannah was concentrating on the highway that ran along the ocean. In some spots the dune grass grew next to the road and the sand sloped gently to the water. Other places the dunes made small cliffs and beach houses had been backed against them. But, everywhere, the ocean was hypnotic, rising and curling into one wave after another, then crashing on the shore.

Godsey's sat out on the water like a giant raft, open to the air on three sides. A large bar was close to the entrance, where Lucy thought she recognized the tall man at the far end.

"There's Haddem," Glenn said immediately. "Were we meeting him here?"

"Don't point, Glenn," Susannah said tensely. "Of course we're not meeting him. This is a popular place. He's probably waiting for friends."

"Should we say hello?" Kit asked.

"We can certainly walk by." Susannah led the way.

Haddem's pointed nose was raised in surprise. He smoothed the triangle of red hair back from his forehead and kissed Susannah's cheek.

The hostess approached. "Is this your party? Shall I seat you now?"

"Excuse me," Susannah said, quickly. "You have a reservation for Mosedale."

The hostess scanned her clipboard. "Yes, Mrs. Mosedale, for five at one o'clock. Right this way. I've saved you a big table, right by the water. The way you asked."

"Uh, Haddem. I believe you met Lucy—Lucy Hill—at the house the other day. Remember?"

"Yes, of course," Haddem answered, and offered his hand.

"Hi!" Lucy said automatically, her mind running on. This whole expedition had been rather sudden. Had Susannah set up this meeting with Haddem? Probably not, since Susannah was following the hostess to their table and Haddem had remained at the bar.

After they'd ordered, Bean talked Lucy into looking over some fishing boats idling on the opposite deck. When they came back to the table, Haddem sat between Glenn and Kit.

"Haddem's eating with us after all," Kit said. "He was stood up."

"Now, that's not exactly right," Susannah said. "His lunch companion phoned."

Lucy tried to keep her thoughts from showing on her face. Who did Susannah think she was fooling? What was the purpose of this meeting?

"I understand, Lucy, that you're an accomplished rider," Haddem said pleasantly. His manner was somewhat formal, like Susannah's. His speech was clipped and sounded as though he had a cold.

"Thank you. Riding's definitely my sport, if that's what you mean. I've been at it six years."

"I've an interesting collection of horse bronzes you might like to see. Perhaps Susannah will bring you across the harbor one day—"

"You'll love them, Lucy," Kit broke in. "I'd give anything to have even the smallest one on my bureau."

As the small talk went on, Lucy was all the more puzzled. Whether this meeting seemed accidental or not, how did they expect to say anything private without being overheard? It would be too obvious to send everyone away from the table or even to walk off by themselves. Had Susannah handed Haddem a note? Perhaps when she'd been away from the table with Bean?

It was easy to see that Susannah and Haddem got

along especially well. But it didn't seem to be anything romantic—more like a brother and sister who were really close. Lucy tried not to stare as she studied Haddem's face. His pleasant smile and controlled manner certainly didn't fit with her idea of a "compulsive gambler."

When the lobsters arrived, conversation all but stopped. Lucy was not only busy dismantling her own, but Bean needed help with the claws. After the luscious meal the warm summer air made Lucy drowsy. Stay alert, she scolded herself. You still haven't figured this out!

Finally, Susannah put down her tiny fork and turned to Haddem. "The children are all excited about seeing the coins. So is Austin. More accurately, he's very impatient. He's still in a lot of pain, so he's impatient about everything. Friday all he wanted to do was talk on the phone to the office and this morning was the same. There was no way I could tie up the phone for a long conversation or talk to you freely. Do you understand?"

So that was it. But wasn't this meeting risky? What if one of the kids said something to Austin?

"What I want to stress, Haddem, is the necessity of getting the coins back to us just as fast as you can. I thought you were taking them to New York last week."

"And I did, Susannah. Charlie Rock gave me his opinion, but I wasn't satisfied with what he said. I'm going back into the city tomorrow, so Austin will just have to calm down. The coins will be back in your hands on Thursday."

"Shall I tell Austin that? I'll just say that we bumped into you at Godsey's, and that you sent him that message."

Lucy almost smiled. Pretty clever, Susannah!

"Do whatever you wish," Haddem said. "I know that Austin doesn't quite trust me, and I've ignored it for years."

"Haddem, please take me seriously. There's a great deal at stake here—even friendship."

Haddem chose not to answer, looking imperious instead, and Susannah signaled for the waiter.

"That's a great place, Susannah," Lucy said as they got back into the car. "Thanks for a super lunch."

"You're most welcome. I think we'll have lobsters at home once in a while. We'll just fix something else for Austin."

"Austin doesn't like lobster?"

"It's not that. He's highly allergic to all shellfish. Now, who's going to swim in the ocean? Pam's house is only ten minutes away."

As they drove back along the highway, Lucy tried to take part in the cousins' car game, but it was impossible to deflect her thoughts. What had Susannah really been trying to tell Haddem—simply that Austin was impatient? Had there been a more important message hidden under her words? Susannah had given Haddem the coins the afternoon before Austin's accident. Were the coins and the accident connected in some way?

Forget the mystery and have some fun, Lucy told herself as Glenn and Bean chased her into the ocean. The big waves were terrific. After an hour it was still hard to leave the water. On the way home, relaxed and happy, everyone sang camp songs—even Susannah.

"I promised you a treat, didn't I?" Susannah said as she left Lucy off at the path to the stable.

"And you really delivered. Thanks again."

Lucy strolled between the trees, prolonging the mood of the special afternoon. But at the paddock she stiffened. Where was Willy? She'd left him out with the other horses.

Hurrying toward the barn, Lucy saw that the sliding door at the entrance was pushed back almost all the way. The feed bin was open, its top resting against the wall. And there was Willy, right beside it.

"Come here, you glutton," Lucy said. He must have put his nose in the "slider" and pushed the barn door open. Ponies were good at tricks like that, but gorging on oats could lead to colic or worse. Just how much had he eaten? She checked the pulse in his neck and felt his feet to see if they were warm. She put her ear against his stomach. He seemed fine.

Lucy looked again at the feed bin. Willy must have had a good time, but she'd evidently caught him before he'd eaten his fill. A small piece of glitter caught her eye. She brushed the oats away and saw a gold coin about the size of a half-dollar. It was embossed with a proud eagle, wings lifted in flight.

Chapter Seven

The excitement of Bean's double eagle colored the next day. Susannah had agreed he could keep the coin until Haddem established its value. Bean insisted that his treasure couldn't be handled, that any kind of marks made it less valuable, but since he was carrying it around in his shirt pocket wrapped in a Kleenex, his arguments weren't convincing.

"You'll lose it, Bean," Glenn warned. "It's going to fall out."

Bean shook his head. "That's why I put safety pins on my pocket."

"Can't I see it one more time?" Kit begged, as they all walked down from the stable.

"Okay." Bean put the safety pins into his pants pocket one by one, as though punishing the cousins for their lack of faith. Slowly, he lifted the corners of the Kleenex and the kids gathered around. Lucy, too, was glad to see the coin again with its commanding bird, two strong wings raised overhead, soaring above the sun.

Kit bent closer. "You can see his feathers so clearly."

"The eagles I've seen on coins always face forward," Lucy said. "The side view's much more dramatic."

Glenn flipped his hand. "Turn it over, Bean." He looked closely at the figure of Liberty bearing a torch in one hand, a leafy branch in the other. "Is that an olive branch or what?"

"You'll have to ask Haddem on Thursday. He's the expert."

Bean wrapped up the coin again and slipped it into his shirt pocket. He began to line up the safety pins.

"I guess he'll tell us how much Bean's coin is worth on Thursday too!" Glenn said reflectively. "I hope it's not a whole lot."

Kit turned on him quickly. "Glenn, that's mean!"

"No, it's not. If that gold coin's worth a lot, Uncle Austin won't let him keep it."

• • •

The next day no one mentioned coins, trying to be patient until Thursday. After lunch Kit and Glenn went off to tennis, and Lucy sat in the screen porch finishing a letter to Ken. He seemed nearer when she wrote to him, and she'd settle for that right now. But this was definitely her last letter without an answer.

Bean, stretched out on the glider, looked up from his book. "Lucy, will you take me to the library?"

"I don't drive, Bean. You know that."

"We could bike there!"

"Can you make it that far?"

"Of course! I've got strong legs from swimming. Is it too far for you, Lucy?"

"Are you serious?" His face told her that he was. Could she really seem that old to *any*body?

"It's okay, Bean. My legs are strong too. From *riding*! Strong legs give you a head start as a rider, you know. They give you a firm grip on the saddle so you feel really secure."

"What about the library, Lucy?"

"Not today. I've got other things on my mind today. But tomorrow, okay?"

From the living room Austin's cane could be heard tap-tapping toward the porch. A high-backed lounge chair was waiting on the patio for his afternoon nap. His personal bottle of suntan lotion lay on the chair arm. The day before Lucy had been astonished by the finicky ritual with which he applied the lotion.

"How are you coming along with Radar?" Austin said when he saw Lucy. "Susannah tells me you're going to show him a week from Saturday. Will he be ready that soon?"

"Absolutely. Radar's been schooled very well, Mr. Mosedale. Brett must be a talented rider."

"I suppose. He's had excellent instruction both in New Jersey and at boarding school. Haven't you seen him ride?"

"I've hardly seen him since the first day I got here. He's probably riding at night to avoid me. Or right now, even though it's the hottest part of the day. But I can tell that he's using his bridle and saddle. And sometimes I see a piece of apple or carrot that Gulliver has dropped in front of his stall."

"I'm not surprised. Next to women Brett loves his

horses." Austin walked to the porch door. "At least that pesky pony's locked up for a while."

Bean lifted his head. "Willy hates it, Uncle Austin."

Austin scowled. "Brett taught that little beast to ring the doorbell with his nose. Margaret would run to the door and a pony would be standing there."

Lucy tried not to laugh, but her shoulders gave her away.

"I suppose it could be funny," Austin said. "But I have no sense of humor where that boy is concerned." He looked down at the bandage encircling his chest. "And after last week I don't think anyone should expect me to."

So she'd been right, Lucy thought. Susannah might suspect Ralph, but for Austin the culprit was Brett.

Austin limped out to his lounge chair and took off his shirt. He unscrewed the top of the brown plastic bottle and was about to smear his shoulder when Margaret called from the porch door.

"Your office, Mr. Mosedale. Should I plug in the phone out here?"

Austin put the lotion bottle on the chair and started for the house. "I've been waiting for that call all morning. I'll take it inside."

Bean looked up as Austin left. "What are you reading about?" Lucy asked.

"The stars."

"Great. Then one night *you* can help me find Orion." Lucy stood up. "I'm going up to the stable. I need to talk to Brett and maybe he's there. If you want to leave the house, phone the barn and let me know. That's our deal, remember?"

Brett's car wasn't in the garage, so he'd probably be impossible to find. How was she going to get him to drive her to the horse show if they never had a chance to talk? Several times, at night, she'd seen the red Maserati at the Stag's Head Inn. Where did he go all the rest of the time? Where were all those girls Austin had mentioned?

What was Brett really like? Certainly less thoughtful and dependable than Ken. Not that she could count on Ken just now! But there *must* be some some mix-up about where his letters were going. She'd called the people renting her parents' house in Connecticut, only they seemed to be away. Why couldn't he phone? It cost next to nothing, now, to call from overseas. Was it possible he'd met someone new? One of those British girls with beautiful blue eyes and rosy cheeks like the Princess of Wales? With the perspiration running down her cheeks in the afternoon heat, Lucy felt very different from Princess Di. Besides, in that pair, it was Charles who loved horses.

As Lucy reached the paddock, Willy walked over to the fence. "Are you pleased with yourself, Willy Wonka?" She rubbed his nose. "You got into mischief and discovered gold!"

Her eyes scanned the ring and the back field. As usual, there was no red car. She walked into the barn and saw that Gulliver was in his stall.

I can't spend all afternoon running back and forth to the stable, Lucy thought, on the off chance Brett will turn up. She'd ride at four as usual, but on Jonah and Frisbee, to find out for herself what those horses could do. Then she'd work with Radar after dinner. She'd swallow her pride and ask Brett to come along.

Lucy composed a note all the way back to the house. She'd say something like:

Dear Brett,

I know how you feel about the mix-up on Radar, but I need your advice. No. I need your help. I'll be riding at eight o'clock this evening. Could you possibly come to the barn?

Lucy

She'd tape it on the door to his apartment over the garage.

"Bean, do you know where you keep Scotch tape in this house?" Lucy said, as she came back to the porch. She glanced over at the lounge chair quickly. She'd spoken quite loudly, forgetting that Austin might be asleep. But he wasn't there. A large calico cat was curled up in his place.

"Bean, I've never seen that cat before."

"You mean Tiger? He belongs to the neighbors on the garage side, but he comes over lots of times and naps with Uncle Austin. They're pretty good friends. Only wait till Uncle Austin sees that Tiger spilled his lotion!"

"You know, Bean, I don't think your uncle is as unreasonable as you think. You two just seem to have locked horns."

Lucy walked to the chair and picked up the glass bottle. Obviously, Austin hadn't screwed the top back on when he'd gone to the phone. There was a puddle of lotion on the porch floor. A patch of Tiger's fur was dark and matted.

She bent down quickly. The cat was breathing hard and barely able to lift his head. She read the label on the empty bottle: *For External Use Only.* Tiger must have licked off some lotion trying to clean his fur. *Too* much, from the look of him!

Hanging on to the bottle, Lucy scooped up the cat. He felt limp in her arms as she walked to the porch. "Bean, come help me with this poor cat. I think I should take him home."

Cradling the cat, Lucy rushed through the shrubs with Bean behind her.

"Has Tiger wandered to your place again?" Mrs. Proskey called from across the lawn. Her voice rose as Lucy came closer. "What's happened to him? Why are you holding him like that?"

"He needs to go to the vet," Lucy said. "He's licked up a lot of suntan lotion and he's not in great shape."

Mrs. Proskey reached for the cat, then rushed toward the house, calling for her husband. Lucy ran after her. "Take this bottle. The vet might want to see it."

When the Proskeys drove off, Lucy and Bean went back through the shrubs. Lucy wondered if Austin was looking for his lotion and complaining about the sticky chair. But when they reached the patio, he was sleeping peacefully. A new bottle of lotion, top screwed on, was lying near him on the grass.

"Will Tiger be all right?" Bean asked Lucy.

"I think so. He was still breathing, and it was only suntan lotion, after all. We'll phone the Proskeys later."

But Lucy felt shaken by the memory of the limp cat in her arms. For a few minutes she sat quietly, forcing herself to breathe slowly. Then she thought back to what she'd been doing when she'd first seen Tiger: planning her note to Brett.

"I'm going to my room for a pen and some paper," she told Bean. "Do you know where I can find some Scotch tape?"

• • •

At eight-fifteen there was no sign of Brett at the stable, but Lucy could see that Gulliver hadn't been out of his stall. She set up a small jump course in the middle of the ring and went back to the barn for Radar.

"All right, white sox, show me how you go for the bit." By now the large bay was a pleasure to tack up. Sometimes Lucy felt he was even trying to help. She led him out into the ring and hoisted herself on board.

After a relaxed walk, Lucy asked for an energetic trot. She went on to transitions from one gait to another as well as straight lines and ring figures at a trot and canter. Radar's pace was remarkably even, allowing her to concentrate on her own position. At the same time the exercises helped the horse loosen up until his body bent nicely in the direction of each curve.

After ten or fifteen minutes, Lucy moved the horse back into a walk. When she looked toward the barn, Brett was leading Gulliver to the ring.

Play it cool, she told herself. Take your lead from him.

"I see you've put up a few fences," Brett said. "Have you jumped him yet?"

"Not today."

"I work Gulliver on the flat for at least a half hour. Don't jump until I've finished."

Lucy bit her lip. "I'll keep out of your way."

Brett walked Gulliver a short while, then continued at an ordinary trot, just as Lucy had done. Each time Gulliver acted up, he reassured the young horse with soothing murmurs and affectionate pats on the neck.

Lucy watched intently as Brett worked for an even pace, tightening his legs to urge Gulliver forward, gently increasing the pressure on his mouth when he moved too fast. Brett's hands immediately softened each time the horse responded. His strong natural rhythm was exciting to watch; his empathy with the animal was extraordinary.

Appreciating Brett's obvious skill, Lucy was better able to excuse his past behavior. Riding someone else's horse wasn't like borrowing their car. Mixed messages . . . undeserved punishment . . . there were so many ways she could have ruined all the hard work Brett had done with Radar.

After a time Lucy and Brett took turns working on figure eights at the canter. Brett was sizing her up just as she'd appraised him, and the tension between them began to dissolve. By the time they began work over jumps, they were talking easily.

"Have you ever thought of showing Gulliver in a Green Jumper Class?" Lucy asked when Brett finished his first line of fences.

"I'm not interested in shows."

"I've been planning on taking Radar to Appentuck a week from Saturday. I thought—"

"You're what! Someone should have asked me! There's no—"

"Hold it, Brett." It looked as though they were back to square one. "We're only showing equitation. Only the horsemanship counts, nothing about the horse goes into the record—"

"And it was part of your deal with Uncle Austin."

"As a matter of fact, it was. I'm one win short of Open Over Fences. Why not come with me and show Gulliver just for fun?"

Brett stretched one arm behind the saddle so that his T-shirt pulled tight against his wiry chest. For a small guy he certainly had a terrific build.

"I can't take this horse to a show, even if I wanted to," Brett said. "He's still unpredictable, like a little kid, away from home."

"Will you bite off my head if I make a suggestion?"

Brett was about to answer when the stable phone rang. "I'll get that," he said, and trotted to the barn.

Probably some girl for him, Lucy thought irritably. Too bad the phone had to ring just when she and Brett were getting somewhere. . . .

"Lucy, it's for you," Brett called from the stable.

It had to be Allison. She'd already had her weekly call from her father. Lucy rode to the barn and dismounted as Brett went back to the ring. Much as she hated to admit it, he was hard to ignore. She picked up the phone.

"Lucy Hill, please. Overseas operator calling."

"Yes, yes, this is Lucy Hill."

"Hold, please, while we connect your party."

"Yes, sure," Lucy said breathlessly. "Hello."

"Hello, honey, how are you?"

Lucy leaned against the wall.

"Hi, Mom. How are you? Wh-what a surprise."

"I wanted to find out how the Shelby Island thing was working out."

"Just fine, Mom. Believe it or not, I'm talking from the stable. I just mailed you a letter yesterday. To Salzburg, right?"

"I'll be looking for it. Is the family nice? Are you comfortable there?"

"Everything's fine, Mom." Everything, except that you were supposed to be Ken. For the next minute and a half Lucy tried to sound cheerful. She *was* glad to hear from her mother.

When Lucy rode back to the ring, the searching look on Brett's face took her by surprise.

"Is something wrong?" he said.

"Yes and no. Would you watch me do the next round? Radar's started to change leads in midair. It's begun to happen lately and I'm not sure why."

She didn't want him to look at her in that intense way, as though reaching into her thoughts. She'd rather let him criticize her riding any day.

Lucy cantered a small circle, then took Radar over the short course she'd set up—four verticals plus an in-and-out. In two rounds Radar changed leads incorrectly twice.

Brett's mischievous grin was back. "I'll tell you what you're doing wrong," he said, "if you'll tell me what you were going to say before the phone rang."

"You go first."

"You're shifting your weight in the saddle ever so slightly. I don't think you feel it, but Radar does."

Lucy started to protest, but caught herself quickly. He could be right. She'd concentrate on that when she was alone tomorrow.

"Come on, then, your turn." The skin crinkled around Brett's eyes and his grin widened.

"Have you ever thought of putting Gulliver on a snaffle bit instead of the Tom Thumb Pelham?"

"I could never control him with a snaffle."

"You may be right. But I think he gets fussed even more with the Pelham. Why not find out?"

Brett looked at his watch. "I just might. Anyway, I've got to go. You know what to do with Radar." He trotted off to the barn.

Lucy was left in a muddle of emotions—confusion over Brett—fury because Ken hadn't called. She'd walked Radar in circles without any idea of how long it was, when Brett slammed his car door and gunned the engine. Lucy felt utterly alone. Tonight even Allison wouldn't be able to help.

Hardly aware of what she was doing, Lucy put Radar away and closed up the barn for the night. As she walked back to the house, she looked into the sky once again for Orion—the hunter with the sword at his waist. Where was he?

Just then Ed Beech came running along the road. "Hello, Lucy," he said, jogging in place.

"Hi, Ed. Say, will you help me find Orion? Maybe I could look through your telescope."

"Sure, Lucy, sure." He shifted from one foot to the other. "But I didn't run this morning and I've six more miles to do. Another time, okay?"

"Okay." Lucy watched Ed pick up speed, then started down to the house. What a drag, she thought. Ken's disappeared, Brett took off, and I can't even find the man in the sky.

Chapter Eight

At nine o'clock the next morning the cousins were lined up on the porch watching Haddem's dock.

"He's heading out *now,*" Glenn announced, peering through the binoculars usually used for bird watching.

Kit looked at her watch. "Ten minutes to ten. Where's Uncle Austin?"

"Waiting with Susannah in the living room."

"Do you think there are any more coins in the wine cellar anywhere?" Glenn asked.

Lucy smiled. "Did you hunt for them?"

Glenn looked sheepish. "Yeah. I went out with a flashlight last night after everyone was in bed."

"Everyone but me," Lucy said. "I went to the kitchen for some juice and I saw you—"

"Good morning, everybody," Susannah said, joining them on the porch. She looked across the harbor. "I see that Haddem's on his way. Isn't this exciting?"

"Maybe the coins are worth a fortune!" Glenn said. "What do you think, Aunt Suze?"

"I've no idea, Kit."

Was that possible? Lucy wondered. It was hard to believe Susannah had had no advance information from Haddem.

When the coins were finally spread out on the coffee table in the living room, Lucy felt strangely disappointed. She realized she'd built up a picture in her mind out of *Treasure Island* or some other pirate adventure. She had somehow visualized piles of gold coins cascading onto the table from a worn leather bag. Instead each coin was in its own clear plastic case so you could see both sides.

Lucy sat on the big couch with Susannah and Austin while the cousins knelt against the other side of the coffee table. Haddem had pulled over a chair and stacked the little squares in front of them.

"Do you have an extra one of those?" Bean asked.

"An extra coin? Of course not, Bean."

"No. I've *got* a coin. I mean the little plastic thing to keep it right."

Haddem was clearly startled. He turned to Susannah, almost as though demanding an explanation. Then all expression abruptly left his face. What was going on here? Lucy wondered. What difference did it make to Haddem if Bean had found another coin?

"We only learned about Bean's coin when we got back from Montauk on Monday," Susannah said. "You were in New York for the next two days. In any case, Amos tells me the box tumbled open when the wall was demolished and a handful of coins rolled out. He thought he'd found them all, but since he was hurrying to hide the discovery from the workmen nearby, one must have been overlooked. The next day, Bean was hiding under the tarp—and that's the story."

"Well, let's get down to business," Austin said. "Bean's single coin doesn't concern us here."

"Austin, I'm sorry I couldn't get these back to you sooner, but I really had to do a careful check. To begin with the obvious, all these coins are twenty-dollar gold pieces known as St. Gaudens Double Eagles—St. Gaudens, after the famous sculptor who designed them, which, of course, accounts for their unusual beauty. Double Eagles because the ten-dollar gold piece was known as the Eagle, so the twenty was 'Double.' "

Haddem obviously enjoyed his authoritative position. He seemed to look at everyone over his sharp nose, and his voice was more nasal than Lucy remembered. "The twenty-four coins Susannah gave me," he went on, "were all from the years 1926 and 1927. That's in your favor since in those years fewer coins were minted than in some others. Now, you know that coins are valued according to condition as well as rarity. For example, look here." He put two coins next to each other. "See the coin on the left? All the details of the design are sharp— the drapery, the lettering, the date."

Bean had practically climbed onto the coffee table in his determination to see the coins clearly. Glenn pushed him to one side, making room for himself and Kit.

"This coin would be classified as 'extra fine.' Now, this second coin is considered to be 'fine' not 'extra fine.' The outline of the figure is still clear, the lettering and the date are sharp, but the drapery is worn in a number of places."

"So what's the bottom line, Haddem?" Austin said. "What are they worth, all told?"

"I don't know what you're expecting, Austin, but the best indication I've been able to obtain is between five and six hundred a gold piece. Multiply that by twenty-four."

In the silence that followed, Lucy tried to figure out what everyone was thinking. Surely the cousins were surprised that Bean's find was worth so much. But they were clearly disappointed at the total figure. Susannah seemed pleased, Austin was impossible to read.

"Well, Haddem, I guess we owe you a debt of gratitude for looking into all this for us," Austin said finally. "Of course we'd have liked to hear some huge figure, but an extra twelve thousand's nothing to sneeze at. Here's the receipt you gave Susannah. You should have it back." He handed over the paper.

"Glad to help anytime. You know that. How are the ribs feeling?"

"Much better, thanks. We missed you at last night's game. Pam Firestone played like an idiot. I'll be glad to have you back next week so Susannah and I can beat the pants off you."

Austin walked Haddem to the porch door. He stood there awhile, watching him walk down the path with the cousins chasing along.

"You see, there was nothing to be concerned about," Susannah said when Austin came back to the room.

Austin looked at her closely. There was a long pause. "I'm not sure. Haddem's worried about something. I can tell."

Susannah started to protest, but noticed Lucy lagging behind. Nothing had been said about Bean's coin. Surely he shouldn't be wandering around with the equivalent of five hundred dollars in his pocket.

"What is it, Lucy?" Susannah said.

"What about Bean's coin? He's taking good care of it, but—"

Susannah waved her away. "We'll deal with that later. You keep an eye on it."

Lucy started for the patio. She waved at Ed Beech, who was walking toward the kitchen with some kind of herb in his hand. She heard Austin say, "Something's wrong, Susannah, mark my word."

● ● ●

At exactly eleven o'clock Lucy found Kit and Glenn sitting on the ring fence where she'd told them to meet her. After Haddem had left, she'd surprised them by announcing there would be no riding that morning until they'd had a talk. They should leave their horses in the paddock and meet her at the ring.

Bean was leading Willy toward Glenn. "Glenn, have you ever seen a frog on a pony?"

"Too late, Bean. Last night I was looking through Lucy's Pony Club manual. I learned the withers, the hock, and the frog too."

"You've got a long way to go to finish the whole horse," Lucy said, more severely than she'd intended. She was disappointed that Bean's joke had again fallen flat.

"The reason I wanted to talk to you is because yesterday I'd been on Shelby Island a week. We're not getting very far up here and there are only about three more weeks to go—"

"Until the show?" Bean said.

"Until I leave without having done my job the way I want to. You're grooming your horses lots better, but once you get on their backs you don't learn anything new. I've figured out why. You've been riding the same horses in the same ring for three years now without understanding what real riding's about. Riding's a skill as demanding as tennis or sailing, maybe more, because your horse is a living athlete, another personality, not a *thing* like a racquet.

"Now, I've a hunch that if you work hard, I can talk Susannah into letting you jump a few fences before I go. But in the meantime I've an idea. Have you ever been to the National Horse Show?"

"Aunt Susannah's taken us a couple of times," Glenn said.

"How about planning a surprise for your parents? They all come back to Shelby Island at the end of the month, right?"

"Yeah, the weekend of Grandpa's birthday is a family tradition. Even though he's dead, Bull Moose weekend is the big deal of the summer. After that we kids go home."

"What kind of a surprise, Lucy?" Kit said.

"How about a special musical ride like the one the Canadian Mounties or the New York Mounted Police do at the National?"

"Just us two?"

"Unless we can get Bean onto Willy. It would be great if he'd carry a flag."

"What do you say, Bean?" Glenn asked.

"Why don't you get Brett to ride too?" Bean said.

"You know, Bean, you've held out on us long enough. I don't think you're afraid of horses anymore, if you ever were. I think you're just being stubborn, and I'm the one who's going to get the flak."

Bean's brow was furrowed and his eyes looked troubled. "Why, Lucy?"

"When your uncle hired me, I made a foolish promise. I told him I'd get you to ride. I didn't think there was a kid in the world I couldn't get onto a horse. I thought I'd just have to help you overcome your fear. I didn't know I was caught in a private war."

Several red spots had erupted on Bean's face. "I'll think about it," he said.

"Think *hard*, Bean. What about you, Glenn? If I work out a really good musical ride, with interesting patterns at a walk, trot, and canter, will you really work hard enough to pull it off? And, Kit, how about you?"

"I'm not sure what you mean."

Lucy found a stick and traced a few patterns in the dirt at their feet.

Glenn studied the markings. "Could we make that look like anything?"

"If you polished up your riding. We'd have to work hard. Maybe even some extra sessions at night. Particularly on weekends, when we lose you to the yacht club."

"Can we start today?" Kit asked.

"Of course. Go get your horses. But wait. You're not to mount until you bring them to the ring."

Kit and Glenn looked at each other quizzically.

"You're going to change horses. Just for today."

"I don't know if Kit can get Jonah going. You've got to get after him."

Kit snapped, "You'll have your troubles, too, I'm sure. Frisbee's a sensitive horse. You can't yank him around."

"We'll manage," Lucy said with a big smile on her face.

Kit and Glenn walked off, but Bean just stood there, holding Willy's lead shank. "Lucy," he said, "how do I get up on Willy?"

"Did I hear you right?"

Bean hung his head. "Yeah."

"I'll tell you what," Lucy said. "We'll do it the right way tomorrow. What if I just *put* you up there right now."

Bean looked hesitant, but he didn't say no. She picked up the skinny boy before he had a chance to think and put him on Willy's back. "For now, hug Willy's sides with your legs and grab a piece of his mane in your hand. I'll lead him to the barn."

Willy Wonka, Lucy swore to herself, if you act up now you'll go to bed hungry.

She walked beside Bean and watched the uneasiness leave his face.

"Hey, Lucy, when do I get the flag?"

• • •

After the morning's victory Lucy was more than willing to cooperate with Bean's plans. Besides, the library was next to the post office.

"It has to be today," Bean said with surprising intensity. "While I still have it."

"I don't understand, Bean."

"*Please*, Lucy."

As it happened, there was no need for the long bike ride. Mitchell, Margaret's husband, had some errands in the village. He dropped them off at the post office and promised to pick them up an hour later.

"You can go get the mail," Bean said immediately. "I'll be all right by myself. Miss Cooley knows me from last year; she'll help me."

Lucy looked after Bean as he ran off. She noticed for the first time that he wasn't returning any books. Then why were new ones so terribly important?

Lucy dragged her feet into the post office. The postmistress handed her the Mosedale mail, and she shuffled through the envelopes with little enthusiasm. A pale pink envelope took her by surprise. It was addressed to Lucy Hill in a child's writing. She studied the postmark. Oakdale, New York. She turned it over quickly. It was from Stacy, Stacy Peister, Ken's half sister—her riding pupil who'd brought them together. Lucy tore the envelope open. The writing was painstakingly neat:

Dear Lucy,

Ken is in Austria with his mother. He is very unhappy because your letters are in London. He called you in Conn. and N.Y. but got no answer. I told him the address you gave me where you are taking care of the children.

I miss you. I want you to see me jumping. The fences are too low but Frank says they have to be that way.

Love forever,
Stacy

Lucy turned in circles, hugging the letter against her chest. She ran out of the post office door and across to the library. Bean was waiting by the librarian's desk and staring at the door.

"Bean's shown me his gold coin," the librarian said, "and we've agreed that you should take care of it from now on."

"Bu-ut, he's been very careful."

"It's special, Lucy. That's why I wanted to look up about it before Aunt Susannah took it away."

"Miss Cooley," Lucy began, "I don't—"

"It's got a D on it for the Denver mint," Bean said. "Here, look in this book."

Lucy ran her eyes down the page headed DOUBLE EAGLES ($20.00).

"See here—1927." Bean pointed. "The plain one's $325 very fine, $350 extra fine. The S means San Francisco. That's $1,350 and $2,250."

Lucy moved back quickly to 1927-D.

"The book's out of date," Miss Cooley said, as Lucy tried to absorb the numbers next to Bean's skinny finger. Thirty-five thousand and $85,000! "I checked an item in *The New York Times,* and I've photocopied it for you. At a New York auction in 1990 one extra fine 1927-Denver brought $420,000!"

Chapter Nine

Lucy and Bean walked out of the library without a word. Lucy felt as though the gold coin were burning through the pocket in the front of her jeans.

"We'll talk about this when we get home, right? Not before," Lucy said quickly. The station wagon was already at the curb. Bean nodded and climbed into the seat next to Mitchell.

Alone in the back Lucy's head was spinning. She couldn't believe the value of Bean's coin. And she was overwhelmed by another thought. Out of all those coins, was there really only one with a special mint mark? If Austin was right about his college pal, Haddem might have pocketed a Denver coin or two.

No, of course not. Susannah had a receipt. He'd have brought back the same number of coins she'd given him. But did the receipt say anything about mint marks? That was the important thing to find out. Since they meant nothing to Susannah, Haddem could have ignored them. Then all he had to do was replace the Denver coins with ordinary ones. He could be making an absolute fortune!

"What made you notice, Bean? How come you knew about mint marks?" Lucy asked when they got out of the car in front of the house.

"At home I've got this great big wine bottle with a handle. Mom's put all her pennies in it since I was born and I throw in the ones I find. I've got this paperback book that says what they're worth. You know the 1926 penny with Lincoln on it? With the D it's worth twenty cents. With the S it's a dollar." He laughed. "But I've never found any."

• • •

Lucy listened for Austin's BMW while she played her cassette recorder in the living room. She was running through her tapes to find pieces for the musical ride— lively ones with strong rhythm. Glenn and Kit had lent her some tapes too.

Susannah walked in the front door. "Why, Lucy," she said, "you're still up. We don't usually see you at eleven o'clock."

Lucy stood up quickly. "Sorry, Susannah, I didn't hear you come in." She switched off the music and turned her riding diagrams facedown. "Is Austin all right?"

"Certainly. He just dropped me off at the door and he's putting the car in the garage." Susannah's face sharpened. "Is something wrong here?"

"No. No, everything's fine. I just need to talk to you and Austin—"

"You do?" Austin said, stepping into the living room. "Trouble with Brett again?"

"No. We've called a truce. We actually rode together last night."

Austin and Susannah sat down at the center of the room. "Well, then, what is it?"

Lucy pulled up a chair. "Here's Bean's coin," she said, placing the Kleenex packet on the coffee table. "And here is an article from *The New York Times* that the librarian in the village photocopied for us."

Lucy tried to sit patiently while Austin read the clipping. He handed it to Susannah, then took off his glasses and rubbed his eyes.

"What made you decide to look into the matter?"

"I didn't, Mr. Mosedale. Actually, I was in the post office most of the time. Bean knew about mint marks, and from the time his coin turned up he's been after me to go to the library. He looked up the value in a book he knew about. And then Miss Cooley remembered the article."

Austin's cheek twitched. "Haddem never mentioned mint marks at all. Not even that these coins were ordinary or they'd have been worth more if—"

"Austin, you've no *proof,*" Susannah sputtered.

"Don't you see, Susannah? You felt protected by the receipt. It said that he took twenty-four double eagles— 1926 and '27. He brought back twenty-four double eagles—1926 and '27. But you paid no attention to the mint marks and Haddem conveniently neglected to record them. Isn't it odd that there was only one coin from a special mint and that it was Bean's coin—the only one Haddem never got his hands on?"

Austin's temper rose with each sentence.

"I'm pained and appalled. The man's our friend. You know what's happened—he's been called on some gambling IOU! I should have realized when the appraisal took more than a week. *More* than a week! He was swapping the coins, that's what took so long. There are only so many places around New York where you can just walk in and get two, three—who knows how many—1926 and -7 double eagles in extra fine condition. And he wouldn't buy them all in one place. That would be too easy to trace."

Susannah's face was as white as Kit's scallop shells. "Austin, you don't know any of this for a fact. You know Haddem's problem about money—so naturally you've made up a whole scenario."

"Do you know what Haddem's going to do?" Austin fumed. "He'll sell one of the coins right away, but then he'll sit on the rest. Let's say there were five special D's in the batch. It might have cost him twenty-five hundred dollars to replace them. Now if he just waits awhile, if he puts them out on the market carefully, not only in New York but in London and . . ."

He turned to Lucy. "Be a good girl and get me a short tumbler of Scotch from inside the cabinet over there. You'll find a glass on the shelf."

"Sure, Mr. Mosedale."

"Tell me truthfully, Susannah. Are you absolutely certain that Haddem is so Simon pure here? You have no doubts at all?"

"I—I can't say that I don't. In fact, Monday I arranged to meet Haddem off island to tell him you were concerned about the delay. I know he's been troubled lately and, well . . ."

"I'm sorry, Susannah. Would *you* like a drink?" Austin said. "I should have asked you before."

Susannah waved the suggestion away. "I beg you to remember that we still have no proof."

Austin took the glass from Lucy. "We'll get the proof, Susannah. I'm certain we will. I'll have a detective tracing the coin purchases tomorrow. But meanwhile, I warn you. Not the slightest suspicion is to be conveyed to Haddem. He'll visit as always. We'll play bridge as always. We don't want him to dart away with that treasure he's hoarding."

Austin took a big swallow of Scotch and sat back against his chair. "Lucy, do you think Bean suspects any of this?"

"Yes. He probably does. But he'll never talk about it unless you ask him. Anyway, by tomorrow he'll be interested in something else. You know what Bean's like."

"Well, Lucy, it's late. I'm sure you'd like to get some sleep. Thank you for waiting up and letting us know this news as soon as possible."

"You're welcome." She left the room briskly. It was irritating to be dismissed like a child. After all, she'd discovered the truth about the accident in the boathouse before anyone else.

Back in her room Lucy began to think. The accident in the boathouse had happened the day after Susannah consulted Haddem about the coins. With Austin out of the way Haddem might have offered her a split. But Susannah was no murderer! Anyway, nothing at all had happened since—not unless you counted a sick cat. Lucy reached for the bedpost. No one would have tested the contents of the lotion bottle. Plain ordinary suntan lotion was enough to get Tiger into trouble. But what if there had been something poisonous in the bottle, something that could be absorbed through the skin?

Lucy, you're taking off like Austin now, she scolded. That bottle went out in the vet's trash long ago, so forget it.

She stretched out on her bed, ready to forget about mysteries altogether. Stacy's letter had ended her misery about Ken. She could just let go and remember his strong arms, the softness in his eyes as his face came close. She fell asleep across the bed before she'd even brushed her teeth.

* * *

Lucy awoke with a start. Was that a knock on her door?

"Lucy?"

Who was that?

"Lucy. It's Brett. Open the door."

The red numbers on her clock read a few minutes after one. She got up and went to the door.

"Its very late, Brett."

"Lucy, hurry. Grab some clothes and come out here."

Brett could be mean when he'd been drinking. She could hear the slur in his voice.

"Come on, Lucy. There's something you'll want to see."

Curiosity took over. She pulled on a pair of jeans, slipped into a shirt, and opened the door.

"Come quick, but be very quiet." Brett led the way to the front door, opened it softly, and stepped outside. "Bean said you wanted to see a deer."

A beautiful doe stood next to the vegetable garden, her fawn beside her. Several yards away a large buck held his head high. Lucy was thrilled. She and Brett stood together on the steps without a word. When the animals bounded off, Lucy let out her breath.

"Thanks, Brett. That was worth getting up for."

"I was walking around by myself after I put the car away. When I came back to the steps here, I saw them." For a moment his expression was surprisingly sad, but he replaced it quickly with a roguish smile. "How about some coffee in the kitchen? Margaret's got some good apple pie in the fridge too."

Lucy followed him to the kitchen.

"Dig into this," Brett said as he put a huge wedge of pie on the table. "Want some rum raisin ice cream on top?" He peered into the freezer. "There's strawberry too."

"This is great. Aren't you going to join me?"

"I'm waiting for the coffee to heat."

Lucy started the pie and tried to think of something to talk about besides horses.

Brett stood by the stove. "Well, what do you think of the Mosedale clan?" he said scornfully. "Those of us you've met so far."

"I'm having a very good time here. Everyone's been friendly and considerate. The kids are great."

"You can't get to know people in a month."

"I suppose not. But you asked me what I thought."

Brett fiddled with the size of the flame under the coffeemaker. He stared at the glass container for a very long time, as if it were truly remarkable. Then he turned to Lucy abruptly. "I hate their money. I hate the power it gives them over people. And Austin uses it. Boy, does he ever."

"You've got plenty of money too. And—" She paused, but couldn't resist: "You love to spend it."

"Sure I do. Why not? That's one way to get rid of it before it makes me like them."

"Come on, Brett. I don't think that makes sense."

"Besides, it's stolen money," he mumbled, turning back to the coffee. He filled a mug and joined her at the table.

This time the silence stretched on. Lucy attacked her pie. What could he possibly mean?

"You've got your uncle mixed up with Judge Trabert, haven't you?" she said lightly, hoping to get him started again.

Brett looked directly into her face, his eyes now oddly bright. "When I was about Glenn's age there was a law-suit against Mosedale Industries. There was this man, Richard Waters, who'd invented a little thing that improved our safety brake. They use safety brakes everywhere, you know—from the lawn mower to printing presses a couple of stories tall. Well, Waters claimed he invented the *Gismo* and that Austin stole it."

"What did Austin say?"

"He never denied Waters invented the thing. But Austin said he'd paid Waters ten thousand dollars for it and that was that. The company made millions, and the guy didn't even get a royalty. Not a penny more than ten thousand dollars."

"Why did Waters accept the deal in the first place?"

"He worked for Mosedale Industries and I guess he wanted to keep his job. It got very complicated. Waters said he invented the gismo on his own time. Austin didn't agree. I tried to follow the trial in the papers. And of course I heard Austin and Susannah talk about it. Austin said ten thousand dollars was a lot of money at the time and that he could have ended up with something worthless. He said the company had to change the device to make it work. I don't know if that's true or not. But I think he made too tough a deal and that he could have given the man something more."

"Maybe you feel that way because you think Austin's too tough with *you.*"

"Don't give me that psychiatrist stuff. I've heard Austin do business on the phone since I was old enough to understand English. He's plenty tough with *everyone.*"

"Who won the lawsuit in the end?"

"Austin. But what would you expect? How could Waters match the lawyers Austin could pay for? Do you know what happened to Waters? He killed himself a few years later. He had a couple of kids too—a teenage boy and a girl. I think Austin did soften up and send the girl through college."

"Don't you see how unfair you are? You don't know for sure that Austin was wrong. And you never give him points for anything good, but you double the black marks every chance you get."

Brett stared into his coffee cup. After a while he looked up at Lucy. "I don't expect you to believe me. And maybe I see it all in back and white, but one thing's sure, losing two parents and ending up with Austin in control of my life was no great shakes."

"But Susannah was there, too, right? You seem very close to her."

"Yeah, in New Jersey her house is on the same property with Austin's. She was around until Austin got married again and sent me to boarding school. Susannah's okay. Austin uses money to get his way. Money and coldness. Susannah uses kindness, and at least that's better."

Lucy pushed her plate away. Brett was smart and so much of what he said sounded so—so logical, but at the bottom of it all, wasn't he making a lot of excuses?

"Why does Austin matter so much?" Lucy said impatiently. "What if Austin was too tough or Susannah too easy? Why does it make a difference anymore? You're not a kid. You can do what you want."

Brett got up and took a bottle of beer from the refrigerator. As he poured it at the table, he said, "Austin controls my money until I'm thirty-five."

"You could make money. Maybe not enough for cars and horses, but if you hate—"

"I suppose, but at what? And why bother when I've got so much of it? It was my tough luck that my parents made Austin my guardian. Susannah would have been much better. I can get around her."

"Brett, that's an awful thing to say."

"Is it? It's true all the same."

Lucy pushed back her chair. "Maybe you should try

to know Austin better, now that you're older. Especially since you're stuck with things the way they are."

"Unless something happens to Austin." He tilted his head back and drained the beer bottle.

"Who handles your money then?"

"Susannah, of course." He hurled the bottle to the wastebasket with deadly aim.

Chapter Ten

"Say, Austin, what happened to your cruise?" Ed Beech called from the foot of the dock as Lucy and Bean followed Austin to the *Gismo*. "I thought you were taking some friends up to Block Island."

"The Paynes had to cancel. Want to come along? We need help with the extra sandwiches."

"Where are you going?" Ed walked out toward the boat.

"The horses rest today, so we thought we'd get Lucy on the high seas. Put a fishing pole in her hands for a change."

"I'm going to teach her to bait a hook," Bean said.

"I thought you had a date with me, Bean. Weren't we going bird watching?" Ed said. "Lucy can come along too."

Bean looked at his feet. "It wasn't so sure."

"It's a scorcher today. You're going to broil out there."

"We'll be okay." Bean climbed onto the boat.

Ed watched them load the boat for a while, then

walked away. Lucy thought he seemed rather lonely. She saw him alone most mornings when she went up to the stable and he jogged along the road. She couldn't remember any company at his house since she'd been here, besides the Mosedale cousins.

Mitchell arrived with the lunch and the bait pail, then threw the stern line to Austin. Austin backed the *Gismo* away from the dock, turned the wheel hard, and headed for the open water.

In a fishing chair at the stern Lucy relaxed with the motion of the boat and held up her face to the wet salt air. Bean scrambled around on the gunwale and worked his way forward to the bow. Perched there, he looked like a skinny figurehead in navy swim trunks and an orange life jacket.

When they left the harbor, Lucy climbed onto an extra stool near Austin at the helm. They sat together quietly, watching the *Gismo* plow into the open water. Finally Austin said, "She's a beautiful boat, don't you think? Oak framed with cedar planks. We started from an old lobsterman's hull and added the flying bridge."

"I don't know much about boats," Lucy said, "but this one looks perfect to me."

Austin smiled happily. "She's got plenty of power too." He looked ahead to the bow. "How are you getting along with that young man up there? Is he still holding out on us?"

"We're getting there," Lucy said. She wasn't going to ruin the surprise.

"I tell Katherine she isn't tough enough with him. We don't need another Brett on our hands."

For a moment Lucy hesitated. But it was somehow

easier to speak up to Austin out here in the open. "I didn't know Brett as a kid, Mr. Mosedale, but he seems to me like a very different sort of person from Bean."

"That's because Brett was spoiled rotten. From the time his parents died, Susannah's given him everything he wanted, from a pony to a sports car. I suppose Brett was the closest to a son she was going to get, but she'd never train her horses that way, I can tell you. If I tried to get close to the boy, she was always there in between—"

"Mr. Mosedale—"

"You call my sister Susannah. Why are you so formal with me? My name is Austin."

Lucy laughed to herself. *I call you Austin already. Somehow it switches to Mister when you're nearby.*

"I'll try to remember," she said with a smile. "Anyway—I don't know about Susannah, but my riding teacher, Mr. Kendrick, used to tell us all the time, 'You can't treat all horses the same.' You have to correct a sensitive horse when he makes a mistake, but you can do it gently. With a horse who's stubborn or lazy, you've got to be firmer to make sure that he learns."

"Bean's the sensitive type, is that what you're trying to tell me? Well, you have to be tough in this world. Bean is too much of a dreamer. His head's in the clouds."

Austin's face was set as he watched the water ahead. Should she say what she thought? Austin didn't like to be crossed.

"Bean's got a big imagination," Lucy said slowly, "but I don't think he's a dreamer. He didn't just admire his coin and dream that it was worth millions of dollars. He got himself over to the library and found out the truth."

She might as well say it all.

"Bean *is* tough, only in a special way. He doesn't think he has to be like anyone else but Bean. When you fight him, he just gets stubborn. But if you're his friend and you really listen to what he thinks, he'll try to do whatever you want." Lucy looked down at her lap and back at Austin. "I—I'm sorry I made a speech."

Austin stared at the water. "Is that how you got him onto a horse?" he said after a while.

"Yes, I guess it is."

"And Brett. Is that what I should try with him?" Now his voice was challenging.

Lucy took a deep breath. "I think Brett just needs a good kick in the butt."

Austin threw his head back and laughed loudly. "You learned all this riding horses?"

"Mostly."

Austin checked the compass and rubbed his chin. "In a lot of ways Bean reminds me of myself when I was a boy. All that sensitive stuff was knocked out of me, and I'd like to see him shape up too.

"People say Glenn is my carbon copy. He'll probably run Mosedale Industries someday and do a good job of it. But if Bean would shape up, he'd take the company another distance . . . the same way I've been able to do. . . ."

Lucy knew she shouldn't say anything more. It wouldn't do any good anyway. She thought back to the conversation with Mr. Kendrick she'd mentioned to Austin. The horse she'd ridden for six months had been sold and she was starting with another. "Don't expect Buttons to behave like Caesar," Mr. Kendrick had said, "and then wonder why you're not getting anywhere. Go with Buttons from the start. Find out what this one horse is all about. You'll get along better and he'll do more for you."

Lucy looked from Bean to Austin. Mr. Kendrick's advice was easier to follow with horses. When it came to people, your own ideas of what they were like might complicate things—or your ideas of what you wanted them to be!

Austin broke into her thoughts. "Come on, Lucy. Let's run her from the flying bridge. You can steer awhile if you like."

As she followed him up the ladder from the cockpit, she could tell that his ribs still hurt and his ankle wasn't yet able to take his weight.

It was a heady sensation to survey the open ocean from the height of the flying bridge. As they rode the waves, swelling in a rising wind, she could imagine herself on the back of a giant porpoise.

"Take the helm," Austin said. "You can't get in trouble out here. There's no one for miles around. Watch the compass to help you steer. Keep the needle right where it is."

Austin sat down in a fishing chair on the bridge and Lucy enjoyed the sensation of guiding the boat through the water. But after a while the boat seemed to resist the wheel.

"Austin, you'd better steer. I'm having trouble."

Lucy glanced over her shoulder. Austin had fallen asleep.

"Austin, please wake up. The *Gismo* seems to have a mind of its own. I'm doing everything the same way, but—"

"Er—uh, what's that?" He shook his head and got out of the chair.

"Uncle Austin," Bean shouted from the bow. He stood up and clung to the roof of the cabin. It was hard to hear him. Austin made his way to the windshield and motioned to Bean to come up to the bridge. Bean stayed where he was and kept on pointing to the water.

Austin stepped over to the side of the bridge. "We're too low in the water. That's what he's trying to tell us. We're settling." One cheek began to twitch. "We'll go back down to the cockpit. Then you do your best at the wheel and I'll check this out."

When they reached the deck, Austin hurried to the rear hatch. Even under the suntan his face paled. "Ye gods," he said, "we've been taking in water—enough water to sink us." He moved to the front hatch and closed it again quickly.

At Lucy's side Austin pulled a switch above the wheel. "We've an automatic bilge pump. It hasn't been working. It's not turning on manually either." He flicked a switch on the bulkhead panel. "The radio's dead too."

"Come back here, Bean," he shouted. "But hang on to the handrail. The boat's listing."

Lucy noticed that Austin's teeth were clenched and the skin pulled tight around his eyes. Now she could see for herself how far down they were riding in the water. Small shivers started up her neck.

"Get the life jackets in the compartment under the forward bunk to the right. Hurry, Lucy. The motor's just shorted out."

Bean jumped down into the cockpit. His gray eyes

were huge. "We could be sinking, Uncle Austin. Did you radio the Coast Guard?"

"Of course I did, Bean. Now, run below and help Lucy get the jackets. Find something white too."

Lucy opened the compartment as directed and pulled out a life jacket. Then another and another. At first sight they seemed usable. As she emptied the compartment it was clear they'd all been cut into pieces.

A white towel in his hand, Bean knelt beside her. "Come on, Lucy. Bring the cushions from the bunks. They float."

"Where are the jackets?" Austin bellowed at the sight of them.

Lucy held up several orange pieces.

Austin pounded his fist on the top of the instrument panel. "Someone's gone berserk." His whole body grew rigid. Lucy remembered that he couldn't swim.

Now the boat was rocking from side to side as the water in the bilge shifted with the waves. The gunwales were dropping faster than before. Austin, somewhat recovered, lowered the radio antenna and they raised the white towel.

This is really happening, Lucy said to herself. This boat won't turn over like a canoe or a rowboat. There will be nothing to hang on to if it sinks. If Austin is terribly afraid in the water, it will be impossible to help him. Bean might be all right, but how long can I tread water hanging on to Austin in the open sea?

"What's happening?" Bean said, his eyes wide with concern. "Why can't we use the hand pump?"

"Watch for a boat, Bean," Austin ordered. "Your eyes are better than mine."

As far as anyone could see there was nothing but gray water. "If George Payne hadn't canceled," Austin said slowly, "we might have been out where no one could find us. But there are fishing boats in these waters all the time and one should come along."

With Bean out of earshot Austin sat down on top of the motor cover and motioned to Lucy to come near. "There's nothing we can do. There's a hose that brings water into the engine and a second hose that takes it out of the boat through the exhaust port. Someone slit that second hose so that instead of leaving the boat, all the water went into the bilge."

Austin was talking in a strange mechanical fashion, as though trying to keep himself calm. "That's not all. There are several small holes that were drilled midship above the normal waterline. They must have been covered up somehow. Even a white piece of paper taped to the side would have worked. When the bilge filled up, it dropped the holes below the waterline and they opened up. Now water's gushing in."

Should we be just sitting here describing this calmly? Lucy wondered. But what else was there to do?

"Wouldn't you have noticed the white paper before we left the dock?"

"Certainly not on the far side of the boat." Austin patted her shoulder. "You're a great girl, Lucy. I'm sorry you're aboard. Remember, forget about me and try to save Bean."

Bean ran to their side. "We're only about a foot or two above water. You can have my life jacket, Uncle Austin. Really, you can. I'm a good swimmer, you know that."

For a long moment Austin just stared at Bean. Then he forced himself back to his feet. "I doubt I can fix the radio, but I'll give it a try."

The cockpit was now knee deep in water. Bean sloshed his way back to the gunwale while Lucy went to watch Austin. "Uncle Austin, look out there," Bean began to shout. "A boat! It might be . . . It is, it is. We're saved. Lucy, look!"

A commercial fishing boat was chugging toward them. Lucy hurried over to Bean and he sagged against her with relief.

When the boat pulled alongside, the *Gismo* was only inches out of the water. The old captain took over, throwing lines to Austin and Bean, then helping the three of them on board.

As they waited for the Coast Guard, Austin was visibly shaken. "I wish I could put a marker there" was his only comment as the *Gismo* went under.

Fifteen minutes later the Coast Guard took charge. Both Bean and Austin looked exhausted as they traveled back toward Smuggler's Harbor in a small speedboat.

"Come here, Bean, and sit with me," Austin said.

At first Bean stood still, clearly surprised. Then he moved to a place on the deck where he could lean against his uncle's chair.

Lucy was glad she didn't have to talk. She, too, was exhausted and there was lots to think out. But one thing was clear: They needed more than the Coast Guard. What they needed was the police!

Chapter Eleven

The next day began as usual with the flag raising at seven o'clock. But when Lucy joined Austin at the breakfast table, he seemed like a man in shock. Not only had he lost the *Gismo,* she realized, but he'd had to face the ugly truth that someone hated him enough to have made several attempts against his life. And it was undeniably someone with easy access to his house, or even someone in his own family. It had to be a person with severe emotional problems or so strong a motive they'd lost all sense. They'd even been willing to put Austin's cruising companions at risk.

Lucy was furious at her stupidity about Tiger and the suntan lotion. If she'd been a *good* detective, they might have found the guilty person and Austin would still have his boat. A good detective checked every possibility.

She wasn't going to make that mistake again. Lucy ducked through the space in the Proskeys' shrubbery right after breakfast.

"Hello, there," Mrs. Proskey called from the vegetable garden. "I hear Austin's had a catastrophe with the

Gismo. How could that have happened? He's so familiar with motorboats. It's hard to believe."

Lucy certainly wasn't going to broadcast that Austin had been the victim of attempted murder. "I guess it was one of those freak things, like Tiger getting sick on suntan lotion. By the way," she said casually, "I suppose you left the bottle at the vet's."

"I can't honestly remember what became of it," Mrs. Proskey said. "I was too upset. What a peculiar question to ask a week later."

"I was just wondering."

Mr. Proskey appeared from behind the toolshed with Tiger padding behind him. "Hold on there, Paula. I think that bottle's in the glove compartment of the Chevy. We tossed it in there when we left the doctor."

"You know, he's right, Lucy. Come. We'll look."

An hour later Austin delivered the bottle to the police.

• • •

The next morning Austin and Susannah both were at breakfast with the cousins. When the phone rang, Austin took the call in the "telephone closet" and returned to the table without comment.

No one had told the cousins the true facts about the locker "accident" or the sinking of the *Gismo.* When everyone finished eating, Austin sent the kids off, asking Lucy and Susannah to stay.

"That was Detective Ryan on the phone with the report from the police lab," he said. "You were right, Lucy. There was enough lotion clinging to the bottle to prove without doubt that someone had spiked it with poison. Did they expect me to drink it?"

"This is all beyond belief!" Susannah exclaimed.

"Some poisons are absorbed through the skin," Lucy said, thinking of the mystery on her father's TV shoot in California.

"Not cyanide. And that's what the detective said it was. He thought there might have been another substance in the bottle to serve as a *carrier* through the skin. He's going to send it on to a more sophisticated lab." Austin shook his head as if unable to believe his words. "The detective said cyanide can be ordered from chemical supply houses or it can even be made by a knowledgeable person with the right equipment."

Austin was silent for some time, as though he'd forgotten there was anyone else at the table. Then he shook his head again. "I can't imagine that—that *any*one would go this far." He pushed back his chair. "Well, now, we Mosedales won't take this lying down. And we're not going to let anyone destroy our summer either." He looked at Lucy. "We're all looking forward to watching you at the horse show on Saturday."

"*You're* coming, Austin? That's great."

"I'm certainly not going fishing," Austin said gruffly, and left the room.

• • •

After dinner that night Lucy put on some eye makeup and brushed her hair a few more times. She was looking forward to an evening with Allison and another school friend in Easthampton. It would be hard not to talk about the mystery, but the detective who'd spoken to her after the sinking of the *Gismo* had insisted on secrecy. She slipped on the white cotton jacket that matched her pants and walked out to the driveway.

"You look great," Allison said as she drove up to the house. "How are things around here?"

"It's hard to believe, but tomorrow's just two weeks since I arrived. So much has happened, I feel almost like part of the family."

"Not that, please! You've got quirks enough of your own."

As the car faced the Stag's Head Inn, Lucy asked, "What's it like in there, anyway?" Brett's red Maserati was parked at one side.

"You've never been inside?! Come on, I'll show you right now."

"We'll be late."

"No, we won't." Allison swung into the parking space. "We'll just walk through."

The bar and the dining room were on the water side of the large white house, with extra tables continuing around the porch. The rest of the ground floor was a large open sitting area where guests were reading or talking.

As they circled the room a high-pitched voice called from the porch. "Why, Allison Barker. I haven't seen you in ages. Come say hello."

"Wait here," Allison said. "It's Joan Klinger, one of my mother's friends, and she's a bore. I'll be right back."

When Allison left, Lucy noticed a strong, tough-looking man of about thirty-five, standing against a pillar near the door to the inn. He wore a white suit and white shoes, with an open black polo shirt and dark glasses.

Somehow he seemed out of place. She walked past him to the bar, hoping to find Brett.

"Lucy Hill, how come you're here?" Brett said, noticing her right away. "I'd buy you a drink, but I know you'll be carded."

What a put-down. His voice was almost a sneer.

"I was just leaving," Lucy said, turning on her heel. She went to a tall wing-chair near the reception desk and sat there, trying to cool off.

The front door opened and closed behind her. The man in the white suit moved quickly. In back of her chair she heard him say, "I was told you'd turn up here sooner or later. You've been avoiding us, haven't you?"

A man answered, "There's no reason to raise your voice. I can easily explain."

That's *Haddem*, Lucy said to herself, listening hard.

"Talk's cheap," the man in the white suit snorted. "Just pay up."

This was fascinating. Austin's scenario was being acted out right at her ear. But it would be terrible to have Haddem know she was there. If only Allison would stay out on the porch until the men left. Lucy tried to hide herself in the chair.

"Why, hello, Haddem. Have you seen Lucy?" Allison said, seconds later. "She's waiting for me somewhere around here."

Soon Allison was looking straight at her. "Are you hiding or what? I finally got away from those horrors. Let's go."

As Lucy walked around the wing chair, Haddem was just yards away. He stared at her hard, then started for the bar with his head in the air. The man in the white suit followed. Was Haddem capable of trying to kill his old friend? If so, wasn't she in danger now?

"What was that all about?" Allison demanded.

"I'll tell you in the car. Let's just get out of here fast."

• • •

Wednesday Lucy spent almost all day at the barn. With only three days until Appentuck there was lots to do. And it was a relief to concentrate on riding for a while instead of the growing complications in the Mosedale mystery.

She was excited, too, about the kids' enthusiasm for the musical ride and the progress they were making. Each practice session was divided into three parts— warm-up and basic skills, drill on the routine already learned, and then, something new, if they'd worked hard. Five minutes had been the original plan, but the kids were already begging for ten.

The secrecy had unquestionably added to the fun. It took maneuvering to practice at a time when Susannah wasn't riding or Brett either. She'd enjoyed the poker faces at lunch when Susannah asked, "Children, are you sure you need to follow Lucy to Allison's every night?"

The Wednesday-night bridge game was in full swing when Lucy closed the door to her room after a late ride on Radar. She'd borrowed a new paperback she was eager to read, but first she picked up her journal. She finished writing down the story of the *Gismo* and went on to the poison in the lotion.

What had Austin said about "a knowledgeable person with the right equipment?" Lucy's back straightened. A science teacher could buy chemical supplies easily. She'd never even thought of Ed Beech as a suspect. Where would she find a motive? But since her goof with the suntan lotion every possibility was going to be checked out.

Lucy turned back the journal pages to the day she'd met Ed. It was the day of Austin's accident in the boathouse, and she began to remember clearly. Ed had been holding the strawberries. He'd seen the ambulance men carrying the stretcher up from the dock and wanted to know if Austin was all right. Come to think of it, wasn't that odd? Ed's house was a good distance from the dock. How did he know it was *Austin* on the stretcher? Of course, according to Glenn and Kit everyone knew Austin's routine. Ed had been at the McCauleys' guesthouse all the previous July. He'd probably seen Austin out on the water at nine A.M. every day.

Then again, hadn't Ed behaved a bit strangely when they were leaving on the *Gismo* Monday morning? He'd really tried to make Bean stay home. Had he known about the slit in the engine hose and the rest of the sabotage? If so, he'd have been horrified to see his pal, Bean, go off into danger.

Was there any chemical apparatus in Ed's house? Lucy had only been inside once, and then in the kitchen close to the back door. With Ed caught up in the bridge game tonight, this was a perfect chance to wander over to his house and look around.

Lucy crossed the Mosedale living room quietly. The four players were each studying a fan of cards closely.

"I bid one spade," Ed was saying as she left the room. She went out the kitchen door, then doubled back along the stone wall and through the plum trees.

In the bright moonlight Lucy felt very conspicuous as she tiptoed up the back steps to Ed's house and hurried to the living room.

There was an odd sparseness about the place. Of course, it was rented fully furnished and it would be silly to bring many personal possessions for such a short time. However, nature specimens were spread out all over the room. The shell of a huge horseshoe crab hung on one wall. A box turtle lived in a large enclosure in one corner. She scanned the titles in the single bookcase and found them to be mostly elementary science. Was that odd for a teacher at high school level? But Ed had probably owned the books for some time and brought them along for Bean.

Most importantly, there was no sign of any chemical equipment in the living room, or in the bedroom either.

As Lucy doubled back to the kitchen, her heart began to race. Was someone coming up onto the porch? Definitely. Now the footsteps were crossing the porch. She opened a cabinet quickly and grabbed a glass.

Ed walked into the kitchen. "Why, Lucy, what a surprise."

Lucy's hand was on the faucet. "I—I thought you wouldn't mind if I looked through the telescope. The night's so beautiful. Then I got terribly thirsty and I knew where the glasses were because you gave Bean some water one day when I was here. I hope you didn't mind. I was just going straight from the porch to the kitchen and back again."

"Sure, Lucy. Anyone from the Mosedale house is welcome here, the same as I am over there."

His manner was so relaxed. Had he believed her story?

"Have you found Orion yet?" Ed asked. "If not, let's go out and take a look at the sky."

"No thanks, Ed." She couldn't wait to get back to the sanctuary of her room. "Is the bridge game over?"

"Not yet. I'll walk you back. Just let me pick up a pack of cigarettes."

While Ed went to the living room, Lucy scanned the kitchen quickly. A bottle of DMSO stood on the counter. She'd seen it used in a number of stables for joint and muscle injuries. Many joggers and other athletes used it regularly.

"Okay!" Ed called at the kitchen door. "Do you play bridge?" He led the way down the steps.

Lucy shook her head. "I don't even understand it."

"I'm the 'dummy' for this hand. That means my partner plays both his cards and mine. I put my cards on the table."

Lucy tried to conceal her surprise. If she'd only known!

As they crossed the lawn, Bean was standing near the patio in his pajama bottoms.

"Hi, Ed—hi, Lucy. I couldn't sleep."

Ed ruffled Bean's hair and went on to the house.

"Let's sit here and talk awhile," Lucy said. "Then we'll both turn in."

They stretched out in two comfortable chairs on the patio and looked up at the stars. The night was so clear, it seemed you could go up in a helicopter and pluck the stars from the sky.

"Bean, you've been reading about the stars. Can you show me Orion?"

"Not now, I can't."

"You need your book?"

"Don't be silly. It's a winter constellation. No one can see it this time of year."

"Are you sure, Bean?"

He twisted his face in disgust.

"Okay, I was just puzzled," Lucy said quickly. "I'd asked Ed to help me find it. In fact he mentioned it again tonight. Shouldn't he have known we couldn't find it in this sky?"

"Ed knows a lot, but he makes a lot of mistakes too. I caught him in one this afternoon."

"Oh?"

"Yeah, on the bird walk. We were watching kingfishers down at the pond. Ed was saying how the bird with the two bands on its chest was the male. Well, sure, mostly the male birds are prettier, but not with the kingfishers. It's the other way around. I saw it in Uncle Austin's bird guide when I got home."

Lucy was thoughtful. "Well, I guess if you teach General Science you can't know everything about everything."

"That's what I think. He knows an awful lot."

They sat together quietly until Bean finally yawned. "I guess I'll go to bed now."

Alone, Lucy turned her mind to DMSO. Veterinarians used it to reduce pain and inflammation and also to carry other substances through the skin. It could penetrate deep into the tissues. Was DMSO the carrier for the poison in the suntan lotion?

This was ridiculous. She was building up a whole case without a speck of proof. Ed was a very pleasant guy. He'd seemed perfectly calm about her visit. He was a runner and many runners used DMSO. She could find a good explanation for every question she'd raised.

Above all, Ed had no motive. She had other suspects to think about whose motives she knew well.

• • •

Thursday the weather turned humid. A ceiling of heavy air moved lower all day, until there was barely breathing space for midgets. Working out was tough on both Radar and herself, but there were only two days left to train.

Friday's weather was no better. The sky was dark all day and everyone's attention was focused on the gathering storm. Lucy was reading in bed at the first loud clap of thunder. She lay against her pillow watching the lightning outside the window and counting seconds between the bursts of sound and light.

Get some sleep, Lucy told herself. Her clock read twelve-thirty A.M. But there was something intense and dramatic about the storm. She wondered what was going on at the barn. Most horses had no problems with storms, but at Up and Down Farm, Silver Whistle would rear at the lightning and Redford used to kick the walls. She really should check the horses. The air was warm and the rain wouldn't hurt her. She'd just stay clear of the trees and electrical lines.

Lucy pulled on her sweats and rubber boots. She took her green slicker off the hook. As she opened the bedroom door carefully, she winced at the squeak, but none of the kids had appeared by the time she stepped out of the house.

Walking along in the pelting rain was exciting—even the first flash of lightning. Then suddenly, none of it was fun at all. Lucy felt as if the blood were draining out of her legs. That couldn't have been a horse on the causeway! There were no other horses on the island but theirs.

Lucy ran up the long driveway, pumping her legs as hard as they'd go. It was impossible. She'd locked every stall as always. The sliding doors were closed tight. If only Austin and Susannah stayed asleep until she could check this out.

Panting, Lucy reached the stable with a stitch in her side. The sliding door on the left side of the barn was open. Who'd left it that way? Or who'd come up and opened it on purpose? But those questions would have to wait. How many horses were out? How would she get them back?

The horses nickered as she threw on the light and walked down the aisle quickly. Radar was out! Radar, her friend, who was supposed to go to Appentuck in two days. And Susannah's Golden Toy! What could be worse? Lucy breathed hard and wiped at the raindrops running down her cheeks. Could she deal with this herself? Should she have awakened Susannah? It was too late to think of that now.

Lucy grabbed a pair of halters, a tin bucket, and some grain. She latched the door firmly behind her and started for the hill at the causeway. The wind whipped the trees along the stable path and the leaves thrashed back and forth. She tried to keep to the center of the tar road as lightning seemed to shake the ground beneath her.

There was no one in sight as she passed the inn, but suddenly Brett appeared in the doorway. He adjusted his poncho and stepped out into the rain. Why was he walking toward the causeway? Did he know the horses were out?

"Brett! Brett! Help me. Please!" Lucy shouted as she ran. Her voice seemed only a whisper under the sound of the rain on the road.

Below her the water churned on either side of the tar road. Luckily, the horses had veered to the Smuggler's Harbor side. The stones that washed up on the sand were smaller there. It was lucky, too, that horses tended to stay together.

Lucy ran down the hill. "Here, Radar. Toy. Come and get it." She shook the pail as hard as she could, hoping the sound of grain against the sides would reach them somehow.

Brett ran up beside her and took one halter. He reached into the bucket for a handful of feed.

"Be careful you don't make them bolt," Lucy said. It seemed as if he'd had a lot to drink and his poncho was flapping in the wind.

"I'll get Radar," Brett said. "See what you can do about Toy."

Five minutes later Lucy and Brett led the two horses up the hill. Lucy felt so relieved, she could have skipped all the way. She looked closely at Toy's legs as she walked and felt almost certain that they were fine. She'd trot her a bit when they reached level ground. Then she looked over at Radar. Every few yards he was taking an odd little step that spelled trouble.

Chapter Twelve

The alarm awoke Lucy the next morning at six instead of seven. At first she was startled, but memories of the previous night made the reason painfully clear. She'd set the alarm early to check on Radar's leg.

As she walked up the long driveway, Lucy thought about Austin and Susannah. She was sure they had no idea of the trouble in last night's storm. They couldn't see the causeway from their rooms, and there was no reason for them to know even that she'd been out of the house. But all the same, two hours from now when she'd finished her morning chores, she'd have to face them with the whole story.

When they'd brought the horses back to the barn the night before, she and Brett had cooled them out for about fifteen minutes and toweled them dry. Since Radar's front legs were still warm, it was hard to tell if anything was seriously wrong, though the odd little step had continued. They'd rubbed alcohol on the horses' legs and wrapped them in stable bandages. This morning would tell them more.

Radar wasn't going to Appentuck tomorrow, that was obvious. But that was the least of Lucy's concerns at the moment. She wanted to be sure his injury wasn't serious and that Toy had remained sound overnight. She wanted the Mosedales to believe that she'd locked the stalls and closed the sliding doors!

Lucy tossed in hay to all the horses, then went for Radar. When she took off his bandages, no swelling was apparent. But when she rubbed her hands down both legs, the left fetlock—that part of the leg much like the human ankle—was warmer than the right and definitely swollen. The pulse was stronger in that leg too. Still, she thought with relief, this didn't seem like a serious strain. She'd cold-hose Radar's leg when she'd finished her chores. If the swelling was still there, they'd call the vet in a few days.

The whole time Lucy mucked out and finished feeding, she asked herself why had Radar been hurt at all? Who had come out in the storm, unlocked two stalls, and opened the barn doors? Who had turned out the horses and why?

It had to be someone who knew well which horses were the most valuable. It had to be someone with access to the stable. That ruled out Haddem. He would have had to cross the harbor in the storm. More important, if Austin or Kit had seen his boat from their bedrooms, he'd have been the most obvious suspect. But wait! Was there a way to *drive* around the harbor from Haddem's house? There must be.

Lucy brought Radar to the wash stall. She greased his heel to prevent it from cracking and aimed a hose of cold water at the leg.

Radar shifted nervously. "Easy boy," Lucy said. "This is going to cut down the swelling." She laughed to herself. "It will also give me twenty minutes to think!"

What had anyone hoped to achieve? Since someone had actually tried to *kill* Austin, how could two loose horses hurt him at all? She couldn't think of anyone who'd want to hurt both Brett and Susannah. What did they have in common here?

Who did that leave but HERSELF! Was it possible that someone wanted to get her into trouble, wanted to make her look bad so she'd be sent away? If so, there could be only one reason—fear that she could incriminate them in the attacks against Austin.

"That sounds right, Radar," Lucy said, patting the horse's shoulder. "But what have I found out? And about whom?"

Ed had discovered her in his house, where she'd no right to be. The DMSO bottle was in plain sight. DMSO might well have been the agent in the suntan lotion meant to take the poison through Austin's skin.

Brett? Since the talk in the kitchen he'd avoided her completely except to help with the horses in the storm. He'd been drinking the night they'd talked, and he'd undoubtedly said more than he intended. He'd certainly revealed a strong motive for wanting Austin out of the way.

Then why had he helped to round up Toy and Radar? That was easy. He wouldn't want to endanger the horses and she was already in trouble the minute they'd got out.

Again, there was Haddem—possibly, even Susannah. Lucy had already considered the possibility that they might have teamed up to steal the Denver mint coins.

Was there anything in the conversation at Godsey's that they didn't want her to remember? If so, why had they waited so long to take action? Perhaps the detective report on Haddem had come in. If Haddem was implicated, Susannah would want to cut loose. She wouldn't want a witness around who might guess that she was an accomplice.

Well, Lucy asked herself, what did she remember? There was only one possibility—that moment before Susannah signaled for the waiter. Something like "There's a great deal at stake here—even friendship." Susannah had hesitated meaningfully before the word *friendship*. To Lucy she'd meant just that, referring to Haddem's welcome at the house. But maybe she was trying to choose another word for *alliance* or *partnership*. After all, four pair of ears had been listening.

But Susannah was hard to cast as a culprit. Lucy just couldn't buy it. Haddem was a different matter. He knew Lucy had overheard his conversation at the inn. It had confirmed that his financial problems were extreme. Haddem wouldn't want that information to reach Austin —he still didn't know they'd caught on to his swindle.

I've plenty of notions but no conclusions, Lucy thought when twenty minutes were up. She walked Radar a bit, rewrapped his leg, and returned him to his stall. It was time to face the music.

Austin seemed especially cheerful at the breakfast table, and Susannah and the cousins were taking their mood from him. Lucy sat down in her place. "What's the matter, Lucy?" Bean asked. Leave it to Bean to read her feelings. But he'd made it easier.

Lucy faced Austin and swallowed hard. "I need to tell

you all about something right away. I couldn't feel more upset, so I'll just give you the facts. I got up last night during the storm and decided to check the horses. I don't know what made me wake up or why I went out there, but I saw a horse running loose on the causeway."

Susannah clutched the edge of the table. "Which horse, what horse—"

"Let her finish," Austin ordered.

"I discovered that *two* horses were out. Brett was at the inn and helped me bring them back."

"Which horses?" Susannah insisted. "Is Toy all right?"

"Toy's fine. But he was running around on the beach last night and if you want to call the vet—"

"And the other horse?" Glenn asked.

"Radar's going to be fine too. I'm sure of it and so is Brett. We'll have to cold-hose him three times a day for a while—"

"But Appentuck's tomorrow." Kit gasped. "You won't be able to go."

"I guess not. But, please, believe me. I left the barn closed. All the stalls were locked. I can't prove that to you, but it's true."

There was complete silence around the table. Susannah started to speak several times, but stopped herself quickly and looked toward Austin. She was clearly leaving the initiative to him. Lucy was just glad to have said her piece; there was nothing more she could do. The children turned to her again and again, sending silent messages of encouragement and affection. She couldn't look at them long for fear she'd break into tears.

Finally Austin rubbed his chin. "I don't think there's any question, Lucy, that you closed up the stall doors and the barn. You've shown yourself to be reliable in every way. I—"

Kit jumped up before he could go on, and threw her arms around his neck. "Thanks, Uncle Austin."

"Yeah," Glenn said.

Bean just stared at Lucy.

Susannah pushed back her chair. "I'm going to the barn right away."

"I'll go with you." Lucy looked at Austin. "If that's all right."

"That's your job, isn't it? All of you go. I've my paper to read."

Lucy was at the door behind the others when Austin called her back. "On second thought, Lucy, stay a moment longer. Since you've been so involved in the double-eagle matter, I think you should know the last chapter."

"Did you hear from the private detective?"

"Yes, I did, and Arthur Haddem's caught this time. He won't slip out of this noose, you can be sure." It seemed as though Austin was speaking for his own benefit rather than hers.

He went on. "We now have people ready to swear that Haddem went to three different stores within a few days and bought an ordinary 1927 double eagle in each one. That doesn't give us conclusive evidence that he went ahead and made the swap, but it suggests that there were originally three 1927 D coins—four, with Bean's. The rest must have been ordinary coins and he just returned them. When I confront Haddem with the detective's report, I think he'll see the wisdom of bringing the Denver coins back across the harbor."

"Would you mind telling me the dates when he bought the coins?"

"I can't imagine why you'd want to know, but he bought two 1927 double eagles on the twelfth of this month. Then he spent the night at his apartment and bought another coin the next morning."

"Thanks for telling me. And thanks for—"

"Go along now, Lucy. They'll be waiting for you." He adjusted the folds of his newspaper and began to read.

As she left the room, Lucy looked back at Austin, bent over the *Times* with his wire-rimmed glasses sliding down his nose. She really didn't have enough experience to figure him out. But however he treated anyone else, he'd been fair to her all the way.

• • •

Now the days raced along toward Bull Moose weekend. The police detective came around again once or twice, but there was no further sign of anything suspicious. Lucy admired Austin's calm behavior, considering that whoever had tried to kill him was still at large. It had helped to have his wife come back from Virginia in the middle of the week. Jane Mosedale seemed to be a very nice person and she was pleasant to Lucy, but with so little left of July, neither one of them made much effort to become acquainted.

By Thursday Bean and Kit were in a fever of anticipation—about seeing their parents and about the activities ahead. Glenn pretended to be cool, but threw himself into the preparations all the same. Margaret had been baking for days. Mitchell cleaned out the huge stone barbecue on the lawn. Austin leased a fishing boat for the rest of the summer.

All three kids had taken turns with the cold hosing, and after two days Radar's fetlock had returned to normal size. Lucy was now working him lightly and Susannah had found a local show she might get to by Saturday. She'd only be able to enter one class, partly to save Radar's leg, partly because of the schedule back at the house. But that was okay. What was more, Susannah had asked Brett to drive the trailer.

Thursday, after lunch, Lucy and the cousins went to the village store to buy green yarn for Radar's mane that would match Lucy's jacket. They also bought red, white, and blue to braid the horses for the musical ride.

Friday, Kit learned how to braid color into a mane and tie the braids in tiny loops against the horse's neck. Glenn and Bean polished Radar's tack; they did the bridles and saddles for their own horses without being asked.

By four o'clock a cot had been put in Lucy's room for Kit. Mitchell had gone to pick up Katherine, Bean's mother, at the airport. The rest of the household was down at the dock. At four-fifteen on the nose Dr. Glenn and his wife sailed into the harbor on a spectacular two-masted sailboat. "It's a thirty-eight-foot Sabre yawl," Glenn said, his eyes glowing. Bull Moose weekend had begun.

• • •

"Your boots are blinding me," Brett said when they got out of the car at Broad Acres Saturday afternoon.

"I worked hard on them last night."

The show was in full swing. Other trailers were parked all around them. Horses were being groomed and tacked up or stripped down and walked cool. Junior riders darted everywhere, adjusting their numbers, sipping soda from cans, mounting and dismounting, trotting off to the schooling area. In the distance, over the tops of the cars circling the ring, Lucy could see the heads of riders bobbing up and down.

"What do we do now?" Brett said.

"I go pay my entry fee and pick up a number. You could unload Radar and let him get some of the kinks out of his legs."

As Lucy walked toward the ring and the show stand, the dozens of horse shows she'd known all blended into a feeling of joy. Whether a small show like this, with one ring and a single refreshment stand, or a week-long major competition with yards of striped canvas, multiple rings, and booths selling clothes and horse jewelry, a horse show made her feel alive in a special way. Even the blare of the loudspeaker became a pleasant sound. The dust all over her boots seemed a merit badge of some kind. They'd rub it off before she went into the ring.

Lucy tied on her number and walked back to the trailer. As she came close, Brett made a sudden move to stand in front of Radar's left shoulder. Lucy's stomach tightened. She stared at Brett without saying a word.

"Lucy!" Brett said. "I'm sorry! He must have

knocked his leg against the trailer when the ferry lurched. Or it hasn't healed enough yet. You know I drove slowly. We were practically standing still."

"It wasn't your fault." Brett moved aside as Lucy bent to feel Radar's leg. When she straightened up he rested an arm on her shoulder.

There's got to be an answer, Lucy thought. I can't miss this chance after trying so hard.

"If it was only last week. I met a woman at Appentuck Farms who would have tried to help me."

"Maybe she's here."

"I doubt it. There's a big show toward Riverhead today. But, if you'll doctor Radar, I might as well ask. Hang on. I'll be back."

Lucy hurried back to the show stand. Her class was less than an hour away, so help would have to come fast.

"Excuse me," she said to the show secretary. "Can you tell me if Carola Tompkins is here from Appentuck?"

"There are entries from her stable, I don't know whether she's here herself. Let's see. Her kids have numbers 80 through 88. If you see one, ask."

As Lucy looked out over the crowded scene, a young girl in show clothes walked up beside her. "Carola says I can ride the Open class, Mrs. Smith. Can you put me in?"

She'd got lucky. The secretary smiled at them both and a few minutes later Lucy found Carola at her van.

"Why, hello, Lucy. I looked for you at Appentuck last week. What happened?"

"The horse I was supposed to ride was injured. That's why I came looking for you now. He seemed fine when we left Shelby Island an hour ago, but he's gone lame again. Do you know where I can catch a ride? Any kind of a ride that will get me through the In Gate. I can't have come all this way for nothing."

"Is one class that important?"

"It really is! I need that last blue so I can start riding Maclay classes."

Carola started to think. "I brought a Junior hunter over with me that I'm campaigning to sell. He went very well this morning. And reasonably well this afternoon. He's never been in an equitation class but you can give it a try, if you like."

"Carola, I'll never forget you for this!"

"Well, come look at him."

"I guess I'd better get on him too. My class is in about half an hour. Would you have time to help me school?"

"I'll watch the two of you a few minutes and make sure you're getting along. I'm afraid you're on your own after that. I'll have horses in the ring."

Carola led Lucy to a lovely little dappled gray of medium size. My luck's really holding, Lucy thought. And his mane's even braided in green. With my green jacket we should make a really nice "picture." Some judges reacted to that, even though only the riding was supposed to count.

"Meet Milky Way," Carola said. "This is Lucy Hill."

"He's really good looking, Carola."

"Thanks, he's coming along. Here, I'll give you a leg up."

She rode back to Brett to let him know what was happening, then they headed for the schooling ring. Suddenly Lucy heard a shout.

"Lucy. Lucy, where did you get that horse?" It was Bean.

"Where's Radar?" Glenn asked beside him.

"Go with Susannah, kids," Brett said. "Lucy's trying to keep her head together. We'll tell you about it later."

"Get a good spot at the rail," Lucy called after them. "And try to hang on to it until my class. It's about twenty-five minutes away."

And now, Lucy, *concentrate.* She knew that's what Mr. Kendrick would say. As she followed Carola into the schooling area, she shut out everything but her sense of Milky Way and the job ahead.

It didn't take long to learn the problem she was going to have with the horse. On the last stride just before each fence he tended to drift to the left. A firm leg on the left and more rein on the right should correct that, but she'd have to watch every move carefully. Too much correction and the horse would just stop.

When the class was called, Lucy trotted down to the ring, automatically looking for Mr. Kendrick on the rail. Susannah, Bean, Kit, Glenn and Brett were lined up together with Radar behind them. That was cheering section enough!

When her number was called, Lucy brought Milky Way into the ring and smoothly eased him into a slow canter. They circled in front of the jumps and started up the course. The first two fences were perfect, the third less so. By the second time around Lucy warned herself not to let up. She concentrated so hard on the drifting that she misjudged the distance to the last fence. Maybe it wasn't as bad as it felt.

She left the ring to a round of applause. When Carola

caught up with her she said, "Very nice, Lucy. You obviously caught on to his little problem. I'll be watching for you in the next few years—two more as a Junior, right?"

Lucy nodded and started to dismount. By now she could see the kids hurrying toward her, with Susannah bringing up the rear.

"You'd better stay up there a while longer," Carola said. "You're going to be pinned for sure."

Could Carola be right? The toughest competition was off at the big show, so just maybe . . .

• • •

When Lucy got home she put the blue ribbon on the table near her bed, along with the letter from Ken that had been waiting at the house. This had been one of the best days ever. "That's my girl," Mr. Kendrick had said when she phoned. He'd even mentioned a new horse he wanted her to ride. Her mother had called and was driving out Monday to take her home. They'd be back in Connecticut in three more days and Ken would be home soon after. She couldn't wait! She was looking forward to spending some time with her mother, too, and having a good long talk with her dad.

This month of July had been just fine, after all. That is, except for the mystery. Was this going to be the first case Lucy Hill couldn't crack? She wasn't about to leave it at that.

Chapter Thirteen

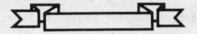

The round of weekend activities continued without let-up. Lucy was glad she'd reserved a half hour on the schedule for a "surprise at the stable."

Saturday evening the cousins had a chance to practice their routine a final time while the older Mosedales went to dinner at the golf club. Allison came to watch because she was going to be busy the afternoon of the final performance.

In the morning Dr. Glenn sailed all comers around Shelby Island on the sailboat. Then a few close friends, the Barkers included, had lunch on the porch. Lucy and the cousins brought plates in and out while Margaret and Mitchell prepared for the barbecue that night.

After lunch Lucy and Allison sat in the sun at the end of the dock. "The windsurfers are like gnats out there," Allison said. "Did you sail with Dr. Glenn this morning?"

"No. To tell you the truth I've had enough of boats for a while."

"Lucy! *Never* put an oversized stinkpot in the same category as a gorgeous sailboat."

"Okay." Lucy laughed. "I'll remember. But all the same, I did some work at the stable instead. I want to leave things in good shape."

Allison looked at Lucy affectionately. "I'm so glad everything worked out well here. It was all so sudden for you and—"

"Allison! I feel like an awful ingrate. I never really thanked you since that first day on the ferry. I wouldn't—"

"Don't be silly. But tell the truth—your stay here *has* worked out better than you expected."

"Absolutely. But there's something on my mind. The family tried to keep the story quiet, but it all came to light when the *Gismo* went down last week. It—"

"You can't keep secrets on the island for long. Dad heard all the details from a friend in the Coast Guard."

"I hate to leave without nailing the person who drilled those holes. You remember the episode with the Proskeys' cat? I was stupid, Allison, I really was. The locker had fallen over on Austin just the week before. I should have thought of testing the suntan lotion for poison right away."

"Who would have listened to you? They'd have thought you were a hysteric or something. Besides, you came here to teach riding, not to play detective. We talked about that at the miniature golf course, remember?"

"I know, but Austin might still have his boat if I'd thought of it. I know what threw me off—the idea that Ralph, the caretaker, had done the cupboard. That seemed like an impulsive move by someone very angry. Then when Ralph left the island for that job in Newport

. . . say, you don't think that job could have been a cover. If he's a sick guy who really hated Austin—"

"He's in Newport, all right. My dad was up there for the boat races and saw him working on a friend's place."

"There was another reason I didn't catch on when the cat got sick. I know some poisons that are easily absorbed through the skin, but even a bigger bottle of those wouldn't kill someone. Now I've learned about substances that penetrate the skin and act as carriers— maybe even for a deadly poison like cyanide. Austin started to grease up his shoulder, but the phone rang before he got very far. And luckily Tiger vomited up the stuff or he'd have been one dead cat."

"So who do you suspect now?"

"That's the trouble, Allison. I can't really pick out anyone. Haddem was the obvious choice, because of the coins."

"I still haven't forgiven you for holding out on me—" Allison grinned. "But then Austin told Dad and—"

"Only yesterday, *after* he had proof. Haddem brought back the three Denver coins last night. I saw them. Austin said his debts are so big he'll surely lose his house out here. Haddem had a chance to walk away with almost a million dollars if no one caught on to his swindle. Thanks to Bean, we *did*."

"It's a convincing case."

"Isn't it? The trouble is that Haddem's guilty only of trying to steal the coins—*not* of the attacks on Austin. We know the dates when he bought the substitute coins. He was definitely in New York the day the cat got sick."

"That's silly. He could have zapped in the poison the day before."

"No. I watched Austin get ready for his nap the day before. I've been keeping my green journal all month, remember, and I made a note on the twelfth because I'd never seen anyone put on suntan lotion like Austin. He was so deliberate and precise, I thought it would be fun to see if he did it exactly the same way every time."

"Okay," Lucy went on, "so Austin always naps at two o'clock. The lotion he used on the twelfth was harmless. Haddem was seen in two New York stores that afternoon; he spent the night in his New York apartment and was in New York late the next morning. When could he have tampered with the bottle?"

"Well, who else is there?"

"I've been thinking a little about Ed Beech—the guy who's renting the McCauleys' guesthouse. It's his second summer here and he's made friends with the family. He's a General Science teacher in a high school and the kids run over there a lot to see his nature specimens and projects. He grows sprouts for Margaret and takes Bean on bird walks. But it doesn't all add up. No one ever comes to the house that I can see—"

"How would you know? You're so busy all day."

"You're right, but I'm sure there's no one there at night. It seems a bit strange that the Mosedales are the only friends he's made on the island. And there's something else. Bean's caught him in a number of simple mistakes—about the stars and birds, things like that."

"Well he can't know every branch of science perfectly."

"That's what I decided. There are other things too. But he's got no motive that I know about. He's pleasant and kind. . . ."

"Okay—move on."

"I suppose Susannah's a possibility. She resents Austin in a lot of ways that I've picked up on. He keeps after her about spending her money too easily. He goes on about how she's spoiled Brett. And Susannah feels she has as much right to run the Mosedale empire as Austin —at least the family side of it. You know how domineering he can be.

"Besides, as you told me, she and Haddem go back a long way. If Haddem had offered her a split—"

"You don't really believe that, do you?"

"Actually, no. I don't think Susannah could ever attempt murder and certainly not where innocent people would die. I think it takes a psychopath to do that—a person who can appear normal and charming but is really mentally sick."

"And so we come to Brett."

"You said it. I didn't."

"Don't tell me you're defending him now."

"I like Brett in spite of myself . . . and in spite of himself. But he's terribly mixed up, Allison. Take my word for it. I'd feel awful if he'd gone this far."

"And you think he has?"

"No—but . . ."

"Who else?!"

"Now you know why I'm so frustrated. I've helped to solve four—no, five—mysteries already. I should be able to figure this one out. It would be a way of saying thanks for these last few weeks."

Allison stood up. "I guess I'd better see if Mom and Dad are ready to leave. Anyway, Kit's coming to collect you."

"Lucy, come on," Kit called. "Shouldn't we get our horses ready?" She was already wearing her hard hat, jodhpurs, and a tailored white shirt to match Glenn and Bean.

"Well, good luck with the drill," Allison said as they walked up the lawn. "The dress rehearsal was a smash. I'll call you in Connecticut next week. Sorry we never got to the sailing lessons."

Lucy looked after her. "Or I'll call you!"

When Lucy and Kit reached the stable, Glenn and Bean were standing beside a homemade "reviewing stand" with red, white, and blue crepe paper wound around each pole.

"It's for you and the cassette player," Glenn said. "We all made it together."

"What a surprise. When did you find the time!" The kids beamed back at Lucy.

Soon the entire family was at ringside—Austin and Jane, Dr. Glenn and his wife, Susannah, Katherine, and even Brett. Ed was there, and both sets of neighbors. Bean rode in holding the flag and walked Willy right up to Austin, where he raised his hand in salute. Austin returned the salute with impressive seriousness; he took the flag so Bean could ride with both hands.

Bean and Willy served as a "post" while Kit and Glenn managed long sets of figures with few mistakes. Finally, Bean rode a small solo at a trot and canter. The lively music added to the fun and the improvement in the cousins' riding was obvious.

Everyone was wildly enthusiastic at the end. At the final canter, instead of leaving the ring, Glenn led the way back to Lucy. He dismounted and reached over the fence for a package. "It's from all of us," he said, handing over the box.

Lucy lifted the lid and blinked as the sun bounced off a small silver horse.

"It's real silver," Bean said. "Uncle Austin helped."

"Read the note, Lucy," Kit urged.

Written carefully, and signed by the three cousins, the note read, *We wish we could get you a real one!*

Lucy looked up. "I'll treasure this one almost as much. I've loved being here." She blinked back tears. "I've a great idea. We'll all go to the National Horse Show together in November."

The scene broke up with praise from all sides. Austin ruffled Bean's hair, something she'd never seen him do before, and Kit and Glenn were besieged with compliments. Lucy was particularly pleased when the kids insisted on putting away their own horses and wiping off every last sweat mark. Then they all went down to the house to change into clean clothes for the barbecue.

From the window of her room Lucy watched Margaret and Mitchell as they went back and forth between the lawn and the kitchen. She hurried into her favorite white cotton pants with a long knit top in white, yellow, and blue.

There must have been thirty people in the living room when Lucy joined them. Looking around at the Mosedale clan, it was hard to believe she hadn't known a single one of these people just four weeks before.

After drinks and appetizers everyone moved out onto the lawn. Tables, bright with blue-and-white checked cloths, stood in front of the big stone barbecue. The coals were a warm red and the big slabs of steak already

brown on both sides. Margaret and Mitchell brought big
pots of soup to each table and began to ladle out corn
chowder into gleaming white bowls.

Lucy was chatting with Brett and Glenn junior when
she realized that something was wrong at Austin's table.
Austin seemed to be clutching his throat.

Dr. Glenn shouted to his son. "Get my first-aid kit
from the boat."

Jane Mosedale stood up and started toward the
house. "I'll get Austin's emergency kit. We keep one
handy."

"It's all right, everybody," Dr. Glenn announced.
"Austin's been allergic to seafood for years. I'll have
some adrenalin into him in a minute. There must be
some shellfish in the chowder by mistake."

More likely on purpose, Lucy thought. She'd
watched Margaret and Mitchell make one trip after another between the kitchen and the lawn. Anyone with
easy access to the kitchen could have found a moment
when the big pots of soup were on the stove. All that was
needed was a container of strong clam broth or finely
chopped clams.

Who *did* have access to the kitchen? Well, the family.
And Ed Beech ran in and out all the time . . . Ed
Beech? Had he been setting up the opportunity for a
caper like this? He was often on the patio near Austin's
lotion bottle . . . near the boathouse too. She'd
thought of all that before, but there had been the question of motive. Ideas began to pop together like paper
clips near a magnet. A real loner . . . mistakes about
science questions . . . a heavy beard and sideburns

even in the summer. Could Beech be someone in disguise?

July had come to an end. Ed would be leaving today. With only one month for his plans he'd had to work fast —three attempts in four weeks. But who could he be? What gave him a strong enough grudge against Austin for *murder*?

"Hey, Lucy. You're miles away." Brett's eyes were twinkling. His smile was mischievous. Not like that solemn night in the kitchen.

Of course! The story Brett had told her that night. A son brooding for years. A son who could easily be mentally ill after his father's suicide. What was the name again? Waters. How could she have missed it? Waters and Beech. Unconsciously, Ed's mind must have made a connection in choosing a name for his disguise.

"Brett," Lucy said urgently, "I think Ed Beech might be Richard Waters's son!" Lucy jumped up from the table and ran toward the plum trees.

Chapter Fourteen

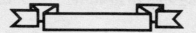

When Lucy reached Ed's house there was no trace of him except the smell of clams in the kitchen. As she hurried down the steps, Brett came running toward her. "He's cleared out," Lucy yelled. "Everything's packed up."

What should she do now? Maybe the McCauleys, in the main house, knew how long ago he'd left. Lucy ran up the back steps. The screen door slammed behind her.

Mrs. McCauley was standing by the stove. "Whatever's the matter? Don't tell me poor Austin's had another accident."

"Mr. Beech, uh—when did he leave?" Lucy gulped between breaths.

"Just a while ago, but why does that have you so excit—"

"Just *how* long ago, Mrs. McCauley? It's important."

Mrs. McCauley calmly put a roast into the oven. "Hardly time enough to make the ferry."

"Do you know which ferry?"

"It was South Ferry last year. We left for Sag Harbor

at the same time. He'll understand that you didn't say good-bye, Lucy. Besides, he'll be back next year and—"

I wouldn't count on that, Lucy thought as she raced back to the kitchen door. She collided with Brett on the steps.

"We may be able to head him off at the ferry. Come on!"

Shoulder to shoulder they ran across the lawn to the Mosedale garage and the red Maserati. Lucy jumped into the passenger seat as Brett slid behind the wheel. When the car circled the hydrangeas, Dr. Glenn and Susannah called from the edge of the lawn, "Where are you off to? What's going on?"

Brett yelled, "We're trying to catch Ed Beech at the ferry. We think he's Richard Waters's son. Call Chief Brown to get the police on the other side to hold him for questioning—about the *Gismo* and the rest. We'll meet you at the ferry later." He gunned the car and sped up the drive.

As they tore down the hill to the causeway, Lucy held her breath. Bounced from side to side, she could barely manage to tell Brett her reasoning.

At the ferry line Lucy gasped. "This boat's almost full and there are three cars ahead of us."

"Don't worry. Those guys can cram on the cars." Brett peered ahead. "Do you see Beech's rattletrap?"

"No. But we can only see the back rows."

The heavy man at the mouth of the ferry motioned to the next car in line. Then another. After that he held up his hand to indicate that the ferry was full.

"I guess that does it," Brett said.

Lucy jumped out of the car. "No, Brett. Come on.

Park your car and let's run for it. If Ed's on board, we'll think of something."

The red car swerved to the side of the road as the ferryman hooked the chain behind the last row of cars. Once again Lucy and Brett were running side by side.

"Hey, wait, Tom, please!" Brett called. "It's important."

The ferry had begun to move, but Tom waved to Brett and lowered the chain. "You'll have to jump for it," he shouted.

Brett took Lucy's arm before she had a second to think. "Go for it," he urged, and they leapt across two feet of water onto the white metal deck.

"I owe you one, Tom," Brett called over his shoulder as he led the way between the cars. "Ed may not be on this ferry at all," he said to Lucy. "We'll check out one row after another."

"I'm right behind you."

They turned in front of one row of cars and started down a second line.

"If you're right," Brett said, "Ed's one clever character. He's been setting this up since last summer, getting to know us all, running in and out of the kitchen with vegetables, part of Austin's bridge game . . ." His voice petered off.

"I guess he blamed Austin for his father's death and decided to get—There's his car, Brett! See? Behind the divider in the single line!"

"Yeah!"

"You must know how to take something out from under the hood so the car won't go—"

"Of course I do, but who says he'll sit still for it?"

"He won't, but I'll get him talking first and you'll have to work fast. Then if he wants to fight, let him. When the ferry starts to unload, Ed's car will be blocking the way. The ferryman will come over to help."

"We'll give it a try. You head for the driver's window. I'll sneak up a few minutes later."

Lucy looked at the opposite shore. This was a much shorter ride than the one that had brought her to Shelby Island just four weeks ago. She squared her shoulders and made her way to the familiar old maroon Ford. All at once she thought of what to say.

"Hello, Ed. I'm glad I got this chance to see you before you left. Why didn't you say good-bye?"

Beech shrugged his shoulders. "I didn't want to barge in with the whole family there."

"I've figured out a different reason. Would you like to hear it?"

For a moment Lucy almost hoped he'd say no. But he didn't answer at all. His brown eyes darkened as the skin around them tightened.

"Are you shoving your nose into something that's none of your business?" Ed said belligerently. She'd never seen this side of him before!

"You tell *me,* Mr. Waters."

"Get lost, Lucy. I'm—Hey, what do you think you're doing there? Get away from there—"

Brett slammed down the hood. The distributor cap in his hand, he headed for the stairs to the pilot house. "Come on, Lucy," he yelled, as Beech leapt from the car.

Brett and Lucy raced up the stairs and burst into the cabin where a big-bellied man with a nautical cap was steering the ferry.

"We need your help, Captain Tolliver. That man down there—he's made several attempts on my uncle's life." Brett held out the distributor cap. "I've fixed it so his car's not going to start, but we've got to make sure he can't make a run for it."

"He could leave on foot," Lucy said quickly, "or jump into someone else's car and force them to take him off."

Brett turned to Lucy in surprise. "Does he have a gun?"

"He could have. It doesn't seem like him, though."

Captain Tolliver looked dazed, as though nothing he was hearing made sense.

Brett pleaded, "I don't suppose you could hold the ferry out here until we see the police at the other side. I think they're on the way from Sag Harbor."

The captain shook his head hard as though trying to clear away the fog. "Now, Brett, is any of this stuff on the level? I've known you since you sat up here in my lap and pretended to bring this old ferry into the slip. You've turned into quite a cutup. This isn't some private business of yours, now, is it?"

"Try me, Captain Tolliver. Stop the ferry and you'll see."

"Well, I guess I'd rather hold it out here than have a fight break out down below. The passengers will think there's something wrong with our engine. But if the police don't come, that's the end of it. I'll take that cap from you if I have to do it by force."

"You won't have to, Captain Tolliver."

"Wait here, Lucy," Brett said, and trotted down the stairs. After a while he came back to the bridge. "Beech has gone back to his car and he just seems to be sitting there. Maybe he's given up. . . ."

"I feel sorry for him, in a way," Lucy said. "Basically, he seems like a decent guy. But I guess he grew up with his father's bitterness against Austin and after the suicide, it must have been terrible. Something got twisted inside. He just had to get even."

Lucy thought for a while. "Brett, weren't his plans all kind of clumsy—almost as though he didn't want them to work out? There was no way to be positive that the locker would kill. There was always the chance someone would rescue the boat. And the poison wasn't so sure either. The DMSO might not have worked with the cyanide the way he hoped—"

"Listen," Brett said. "The police!" He led the way back down the steps as the sound of the sirens grew louder.

In a matter of minutes three police cars had created a barricade across the road. The moment Captain Tolliver brought the ferry into the slip, two policemen came on board.

Brett approached the man in the lead. "I'm Brett Mosedale. The man you want is over there—the third car in the left line—a maroon Ford. Don't worry, the car won't move." He handed the distributor cap to the officer.

"Thanks, Brett," the policeman said. "We'll handle it now. I'll expect to see your uncle down at headquarters." He spoke to the men onshore and they soon moved their cars to the side of the road. The cars on the ferry were allowed to disembark. Ed started to open the door to his car but saw the two officers, guns at their waist, walking toward him.

"I'm going up front," Lucy said. "I don't want to stare. It's too sad." She walked to the other end of the ferry and looked back toward Shelby. Several cars had gathered at the side of the road behind Brett's.

Lucy stood gazing into space until she jumped at the sound of motors behind her. Brett joined her soon after.

"They took him off in a police car."

"That looks like Susannah, Mrs. Mosedale, and Dr. Glenn over there. See! Next to your car."

"Good. We'll explain things and come back together on the next ferry."

"Do you think Ed really taught science?"

"I doubt it."

"What would you have done if the police hadn't come?"

"Tossed the distributor cap over the side."

Lucy laughed. "That's what I was going to tell you to do."

Lucy felt the salt spray on her face and closed her eyes against the sun. How had Allison described Brett to her just four weeks ago? "Bad news." She remembered her first sight of him charging up to Radar with his eyes blazing.

"What will you do for the rest of the summer?" Brett said quietly.

"Go home to Connecticut with my mother. Work on my riding with Mr. Kendrick. *And*"—she couldn't help smiling—"see my boyfriend!"

"I thought there might be some guy—"

So Brett had been curious about her? Lucy felt a rush of pleasure that surprised her.

Brett cuffed her arm. "Hey, I'm glad you showed up this July. Too bad you're going."

"You'll have Radar back."

"I won't be sorry about that."

"Brett, you've been an education."

"Well, you haven't graduated yet. Don't be surprised if I turn up once in a while."

"In Connecticut?"

"Sure. Why not?"

Lucy looked over the side of the ferry at the foaming water. "No reason. I just figured . . . Brett . . . Are you . . ."

"Well, say it."

"Will you ever shape up or are you going to let the Mosedale money ruin you?"

For a moment Brett looked startled. Then he grinned at Lucy. "Do I have to reform to have you as a friend?"

Lucy hesitated. "Of course not. By the way, did you try the snaffle on Gulliver?"

"Yeah. It worked. I guess horses are all different."

Like people, Lucy wanted to say. More than ever, these past four weeks had shown her the wisdom of Mr. Kendrick's words. People were different and often not at all what you expected.

Brett was smiling his crooked smile as they both started to wave at the Mosedales over on the island shore. He could be charming, all right. She might as well admit it, though she didn't see Brett as part of her future. Still, the biggest lesson since her parents had broken up last summer was that the future has a mind of its own.

Across the water she saw Bean standing close to Austin. A month ago that would have seemed impossible. For that matter, Austin wouldn't be standing there at all but for one near miss after another. The future would always be full of surprises. But good or bad, July on Shelby Island had made her to feel she could take them in stride.

PATRICIA REILLY GIFF

writes about girls and boys just like you:

• clever
• cheerful
• stubborn
• mad
• brainy
• average
• happy
• sad